MW01199902

ABOUT THE AUTHOR

Zee Carlstrom grew up in Illinois. They live in Brooklyn.

ACKNOWLEDGMENTS

Kent Wolf and Neon Literary; Zachary Wagman and Flatiron Books; Dan Stolar and the English department at DePaul University; Joe Scapellato, Andrew Ciotola, and the creative writing department at Bucknell University; my beloved writing groups; my parents for losing their shit; Ashley Crooks and Michael Rosenthal for cheering me on; Josh Sippie for opening the door; Mark Lazio for watching my back; CJ Llego for showing me the way; and Lindsay St. Clair, so fucking much, for everything.

MAKE SURE YOU DIE SCREAMING

MAKE SURE YOU DIE SCREAMING

A NOVEL

ZEE CARLSTROM

FLATIRON BOOKS
NEW YORK

This is a work of fiction. All of the characters, organizations, and events portrayed in this novel are either products of the author's imagination or used fictitiously.

 For information, address Flatiron Books, 120 Broadway, New York, NY 10271.

www.flatironbooks.com

Designed by Omar Chapa

Library of Congress Cataloging-in-Publication Data

Names: Carlstrom, Zee, author.
Title: Make sure you die screaming : a novel / Zee Carlstrom.
Description: First edition. | New York : Flatiron Books, 2025.
Identifiers: LCCN 2024030917 | ISBN 9781250365675 (hardcover) | ISBN 9781250365682 (ebook)
Subjects: LCGFT: Thrillers (Fiction) | Novels.
Classification: LCC PS3603.A75364 M35 2025 | DDC 813/.6—dc23/eng/20240709
LC record available at https://lccn.loc.gov/2024030917

Our books may be purchased in bulk for promotional, educational, or business use. Please contact your local bookseller or the Macmillan Corporate and Premium Sales Department at 1-800-221-7945, extension 5442, or by email at MacmillanSpecialMarkets@macmillan.com.

First Edition: 2025

10 9 8 7 6 5 4 3 2 1

For Linda and Steve

MAKE SURE YOU DIE SCREAMING

ONE

We rage out of Chicago around four in the morning, hurtling south toward Arkansas because my mom needs help kidnapping my father. Actually, that's a lie. A truer reason: I've been looking for an excuse to leave the city, planning my escape, biding my time, and Arkansas seems like a reasonably good place to hide. The kidnapping-my-father thing is a new development, a situation I do not entirely understand. Normally, I ignore Mom's calls, but I was pretty fucked up last night, and my phone kept buzzing, and it was after midnight, so I thought . . . well, I don't actually remember what I thought. Remembering has sucked since I got this fun new dent bashed into my skull.

Anyway, we are drinking. We are driving. We are making good time. Once we clear the suburbs, the Stevenson Expressway turns into I-55, and the grasslands roll into an endless brown blur. I've heard Indiana called America's Hallway, but Illinois is Chicago's Doormat—an unwelcoming strip of dirt, good only for wiping the shit off your shoes on your way to the Magnificent Mile. This is the Land of Lincoln, the Prairie State, and while they already burn these prairies every few years, I wish they'd do a better job. Scorch the earth and be done with it. Salt the fields, stanch the rivers, roll Illinois up like a sleeping bag, and send the white folks back to wherever we're supposed to be.

This is the place I am from, but I'm from it like the Asian carp is from Lake Michigan. Invasive and destructive. I am a virus with great teeth, upturned nostrils, overpriced shoes, an ironic fashion mullet, and mild oral herpes. I guess you could call me the World's First Honest White Man, but I don't identify as a man anymore, so you'd probably call me other things first: pale, mesomorphic, alcoholic, workaholic, successful, violent, queer, pessimistic, autophobic, unheroic, semi-effeminate, sexually deviant, socially confused, normally repressed, compulsive, repulsive, and photosensitive. That's an incomplete list, obviously, and probably a bit overdramatic, but I am in the mood for drama. I am floating near the cold center of a vaguely erotic black hole, sucking space and time, trying to find something to hold on to that I won't destroy.

In other words, I am simultaneously experiencing a breakdown as well as a breakup. You might think these two things would cancel each other out, but they do not. If that sounds shitty, it is. If it sounds sad, it's not. If anything, it's hilarious. I am learning to laugh and smile and scream in the face of devastation. Plus, the drama gives me an excuse to self-medicate. That's part of why we stole this car from my ex-boyfriend.

We race down the highway with a cop car in the rearview. An unsuspecting highway patrolman, maybe, but I can't seem to shake him. I can't even *try* to shake him. He's been barreling behind us for the better part of fifty miles, and I can't risk doing anything suspicious or overtly elusive. I slow down, and he slows too. I change lanes to dodge dawdling trucks, and so does he. A waking fucking nightmare, but also kind of amusing. I keep telling myself this state trooper would pull us over if he knew about my crimes, and he hasn't, so he doesn't. That is the logical conclusion, but my father taught me never to trust things like logic or perception or the cold solidity of fact.

My father is a fool, but he is also very persuasive. He has a kind of lunatic charisma, like Alex Jones with less emphysema. I don't know how or why he has wandered away from my mom again, but I do know the word *wandered* makes it sound like he's got Alzheimer's or some other diagnosable excuse. And he doesn't. Not really. There is something wrong with him, there *must* be, but he's been tested many times for many things: bipolar disorder, schizophrenia, OCD, PTSD, whatever the doctors can think of. I'm not sure how he manages to beat these tests, but he comes out spotless every time. And here we are.

When Mom called me from Arkansas, I was lounging on the damp red futon I'd been Airbnbing for thirty-three dollars a night. The futon was located in the basement of a blue-haired elderly woman with sparkly tooth gems, seven large dalmatians, and the questionable business model of running a low-rent motel for the downwardly mobile. My living space was cordoned off from the rest of the basement with floor-length white curtains, like an army hospital. I'd been crashing there for two weeks—since leaving my ex—because I enjoy pretending that I'm still as poor as I was growing up. Wait, sorry, that's not totally true. The real deal is I recently burned my entire life to the ground when I took my vow of radical honesty, and now I need cheap places to hide in case I can never find work again.

Either way, I didn't hate the Airbnb. It fit my limited needs, and I met a self-proclaimed garbage goth who was crashing on the other side of my curtain. Her name is Yivi. She screams in her sleep. I'd bring her McChickens and Hot Cheetos whenever I stumbled back to my futon in the middle of the night, and we'd stay up talking about Freddy Krueger and techno-feudalism. Yivi's twenty-two, addicted to pills, and on the run from a very bad guy she calls *Big Gravy*. She's also great at drinking and my new best friend, which is why she's mumbling in her sleep right now in the passenger seat of this stolen car.

Mom is calling me again, but I'm way too sober for a conversation. *Buzz-buzz-buzz. Answer-quickly-asshole.* I can't safely drink with this cop on our tail, and thirst makes everything worse: my mood, my irritable ass, these headaches I can't shake. I wish I were back in that cozy Airbnb basement, sipping Birthday Cakes in the damp dark, staring blankly at my curtains while Yivi hummed along to the *Love Island* theme song.

Instead, I'm out here, braving the real world while my iPhone rattles on the dashboard of my ex-boyfriend Clinton's BMW M2. This fancy-boy car was a gift from Clinton's CEO father on his thirtieth birthday. Blue paint job, silver racing stripes, sticky leather seats, fuzzy red steering wheel cover. It's an adorable shitbox, terrible for long drives and long legs, but Yivi's even taller than I am, and she doesn't seem to mind.

Clinton, on the other hand, was my malevolent short king. Five-foot-five with thighs like Thor's thunder. A sour German-Irish dude from Chicago's North Side. We met in college. He liked the Blackhawks, and I liked his Mastercard, his Gold Coast apartment, and his enthusiastic alcoholism. We got along because Clinton's family doesn't know he's queer, and neither does mine. Also, Clinton's a big-time liar like I used to be. The difference is he grew up too wealthy to ever feel bad about the lying. He used to tell me I should lie more, lie to get everything I wanted, and he was right. Lying got me promoted, earned me my clients' respect, landed me and Jenny a corner office. But it also mutated into a real nasty habit.

I won't go so far as to say I've spent the past ten years living a lie—lest I seem a humongous cliché—but I will say I've been living a few thousand of them. Big ones, small ones, fat ones, tall ones. A never-ending semi-Seussian litany of tactical falsehoods. But that's all over now, and I might even be glad. Approaching happy. Another humongous cliché is the truth will set you free, but that one, I've recently learned, is horseshit. What the truth will *actually* do is tank your career, eradicate your remaining interpersonal relationships, bash your skull in with a baseball bat, and *then* set you free.

When my phone rings for the tenth time in three minutes, I snatch it off the dashboard and throw it hard into the backseat. I am not an athlete, and my aim definitely sucks, so the phone hits the rear windshield and careens around before settling somewhere out of sight.

Yivi snorts awake. "The fuck was that sound?" she asks, pulling her cheek off the window she's been dozing against.

I casually adjust my grip on the steering wheel as if I am a perfectly chill person who never throws Apple products. "Good morning," I say.

"Did something hit the car, babe?"

"Yes," I say, which is technically an honest statement. "Did you have a nice nap?"

"Not really," she says. "Mostly nightmares. Are we there yet?"

"Any cowboy guys?" I ask, because, well, I'm just remembering this, but Yivi's last nightmare is the reason we left Chicago in such a hurry this morning. We spent most of the past few days rewatching old movies—*Thelma and Louise, Lost in Translation, Pulp Fiction, Drugstore Cowboy, The Parent Trap, Stand by Me, Alien, Finding Nemo, Deliverance,* and *Apocalypse Now* in that order—and drinking as much as we could without throwing up. Yivi eventually did throw up, and it was right around then that she got very serious, speaking with a haunted affect as she described her nightmare by the light of my glowing laptop screen. I'm used to Yivi talking about her dreams because she's a weirdo like that, but this dream was different. It was about me and her, the two of us hiding in that basement, and a cowboy with a tan truck parked in front of the Airbnb. She said the cowboy with the tan truck was someone she recognized, someone who worked for Big Gravy, and when I looked out the grimy half-moon basement window, I swear to Todd I saw a guy wearing a cowboy hat leaning against a telephone pole, just lurking there, waiting for something. Then my mom called, and I felt like, in that moment, I needed to answer. My life has been pretty wild lately, and while I don't believe in shit like fate or precognition, Yivi certainly does, and we got rolling pretty quick after Mom said she needed my help.

"Cowboy guy was there, yeah," Yivi says. "And so were some cops." She reaches for the nearly empty bottle of Disaronno jiggling in the cupholder, but I swat her hand.

"Don't," I say. "There's a state trooper right behind us."

"There is?"

"Don't fucking look back there."

"If they wanted to pull us over, they'd pull us over."

"But you literally just said you had a dream about cops." I glance at my lanky psychic friend as she flips open the visor mirror and smoothes her bleached eyebrows. Neither of us has showered in days, and Yivi's dark curly hair is an oil spill over the sides of her long, tan face. Smeared black mascara paints rings around the rosies of her bloodshot eyes. Her black silk shirt is rumpled, her black schoolgirl skirt is stained, and her whole Sailor-Moon-on-the-way-to-a-funeral vibe is a tad bit freakshow, but she's still the most stunning person I've ever met. Beautiful the way needles are beautiful—long and slight and sharp. Her nose is vicious, her mouth is brutal, her everything else screams *handle with care.*

"Don't look at me, babe," she says, closing the visor. "I'm a goblin—and not even the sexy kind."

"Yivi. The *cops.* What happened in your dream?"

"They def didn't pull us over on the highway."

"I need you to tell me right now where you saw them," I say, making a particularly gallant effort to suppress the hair-trigger temper I inherited from my father. I don't enjoy inflicting my anger on others, even if they deserve it. And Yivi doesn't deserve it. I haven't told her that I'm currently wanted for murder in addition to our casual grand theft auto, but I would still prefer if she'd take her police-related premonitions as seriously as I am.

"Relax, baby-babe," she says. "The cops were in a parking lot."

"*Which* parking lot?"

"Who knows. It was all very fuzzy. And it's the cowboy guy we've gotta watch out for."

"I know, Yivi. I am. But I haven't seen him."

"Then we're goody like Woody." She reaches down between her legs to dig through the duffel bag of supplies she swiped from our Airbnb. All the liquor from our blue-haired host's kitchen cabinets, a box of Nabisco saltines, and a scratchy roll of Scott toilet paper in case we need to shit in a bush. The booze is trash—a half liter of Holland House sherry cooking wine, three Miller Lites, the Disaronno we've been nipping all morning, and a premixed margarita situation courtesy of Señor Jose Cuervo himself—but I'm not complaining. My tastes approach snooty when it comes to restaurants, clothes, and cinematic experiences. With alcohol, however, the ends justify the flaves.

"What kinda monster doesn't keep real snack foods in their kitchen?" Yivi asks as she pops open a sleeve of saltines and pushes one into her mouth.

"The kind who makes you pay money to sleep on futons."

"Blechity blech." Yivi returns the crackers to the booze bag. "I can't believe people eat these by choice."

"I used to like them when I was growing up."

"Sounds like a sad story," Yivi says. "And I think your phone is ringing."

"I know."

"It's lying on the floor behind you."

"I know that too."

"You're so weird." She spins and flops into the backseat, scuffing her nasty Doc Martens all over the dashboard.

"*Yivi!*" I say her name like a swear. "That cop can literally see you."

"I'm still wearing my seatbelt, safety Sally." She wriggles around until she's facing forward once more, staring at my iPhone screen. "It's your mom," she says.

"I can't talk to her right now."

"Why not?"

I shrug in response. My head throbs. I fight the urge to grab the Disaronno and chug. I genuinely like Yivi, I do, and sometimes it feels like I've known her longer than two weeks, but we have a good-time relationship. We keep things light, easy, sloppy.

She doesn't know my past or my problems, and I'd prefer to keep it that way.

"I don't love when you get like this," she says.

"Like what?"

She taps a black-polished fingernail against her black-painted lips. "Sober," she says.

I snort a laugh. "Same."

"I just don't see why you're dodging your mom when we're literally going to see her."

"She's a rude and whiny neurotic, Yivi. I told her we're coming, and we are. There is nothing to discuss, and talking to her won't help my headache."

"True true." Yivi unzips the yellow JanSport fannypack she's got cinched around her waist. It's a battered bag, and it clashes with her entire gothic vibe, but she never takes it off. "Though we both know there's a surefire way to turn all your bad feelies into good feelies," she says.

"I'm not taking any of those," I say as Yivi tugs an orange pill bottle out of her bag. It's the normal Walgreens prescription type, but the label fell off a long time ago, and it's filled with Q—a freaky designer drug Yivi used to sell with Big Gravy.

"Your loss, babe." Yivi shakes a small red Q tablet into her palm. "I, on the other hand, am overdue for a dose." She pops the pill and affects a Texan accent that would 100 percent offend Matthew McConaughey: "Just lemme know when you wanna start L-I-V-I-N."

I sniff the edge of a saltine and decide food's for losers. This morning's got me thinking about my father a lot: the way he used to say his parents couldn't afford bread, the way he claimed they made all their sandwiches on crackers, the way he always made my brother and me eat saltines with creamed chipped beef for dinner because he wanted us to taste *real poverty*. He called that meal *shit on a shingle*. If my brother and I didn't pretend to enjoy it, he'd lose his mind. But that isn't why I'm not eating right now. The truth is I haven't eaten in almost two weeks, and I'd prefer to think of my self-imposed starvation as a diet. I suck down a dangerous number of calories drinking a fifth of whatever a day, and I need to watch what I eat to maintain my sexy figure.

"Not super appetizing, are they, my good babe?" Yivi says when I cram the cracker sleeve into the pocket of my door.

"I'm not hungry," I say.

"Bullshit. You're starving. And I think we should stop for pancakes."

"I wish." I adjust my waistband where my black Beams Plus jeans are digging a mottled red line into my bloated gut. It's only 7:17, but I'm already very fucking sick of driving. The trip from Chicago to Hookville, Arkansas, is thirteen hours, which means we've still got around ten brutal hours to go. Plenty of time for the state trooper behind us to run the plates on our hot little M2, waxed and gleaming in the flat morning light, and way more eye-catching than most of the farm-country jalopies out here in the treeless middle of nowhere. "But I'm not stopping for anything other than gas," I say.

"Gas always lives near pancakes," Yivi says.

"We've still got a quarter tank."

"Cracker Barrel!"

"Later."

"Death to fascists!"

"Yivi."

"YOU GET WHAT YOU SETTLE FOR!"

"Please stop shouting," I say, switching my right hand to the steering wheel so I can massage my temple with my left. I don't feel like explaining this to Yivi, but if it weren't for the cops, I wouldn't mind stopping. The reality is I don't want to go to Arkansas. Mom is lucky I answered last night. She is lucky I'm on my way. I haven't spoken to my father since we came to blows on Thanksgiving. This was eight or so years ago, back when I was around Yivi's age, shortly after Trump beat Hillary. For a while, I thought I'd grown out of that anger, but I am beginning to see it has followed me. Everything follows me. Everywhere I go, there the fuck I am. The homicidal gender-fluid freako your alt-right rep warned you about. To be clear, I am mostly joking. I am not actually a psycho. I am just angry about lots of things—the wars, the courts, the fascists, the economy, the sneakerhead fucksticks I used to call coworkers. I want things to be different, and that desire makes it difficult to love or like or even tolerate other Americans. But my anger usually aims in. I feel it like sores that won't burst. I carry it like a festering fetus this country won't let me abort. I rarely lash out, and when I do, I prefer Dos Equis. I was drunk when I fought my father. I was drunk when Clinton attacked me. I will most likely be drunk when I wrap this car around a tree. Inevitability is inevitable, and I am losing control. The pain in my head has become my only truth. I think my brain is bleeding. Whenever I dare to sleep, I wake up to the sound of hard wet heat, like hurricane rain, pounding at the drumheads of my ears. And while I'm terrified to see my father, my relationship with Mom isn't much better. After basking in the carcinogenic sunshine of that unstable woman's love for most of my youth, I managed to go from golden boy to black sheep in record time, and I figure she'll like me even less now that I'm a homeless, unemployed, mullet-headed genderqueer.

"My bad, babe." Yivi giggles, and I remember we were talking. "But I'm willing to bet your head lowkey wouldn't hurt so bad if you ate something," she says.

"I've tried that."

Yivi hesitates. She tugs at the white ceramic cat-head necklace she always fiddles with when she's thinking. It's a hideous and whimsical piece of jewelry that clashes with literally all her outfits. I have considered asking why she wears this cat head, but I've got a hunch the reason is sentimental. She'll open up, and then I, in turn, will be expected to reciprocate with some sad-sack story about my father breaking my nose or Jenny dying in a Cleveland hotel room. If you want to learn the truth about other people, it helps to tell them convincing lies about yourself. And I guess I can't do that anymore. "What if it's my treat?" she asks, finally, as if this proposition is in any way tempting.

"You're broke, Yivi," I say.

"But I'll give you a head start when we skip the check."

"We are not doing any more crimes."

"Stealing from corporations isn't a crime."

"It is if you get caught."

"Literally *who* gets caught dining and dashing?"

"I'm serious."

"So am I, babe. I know what I'm doing. Don't treat me like some basic yuppie chick who's never been around any blocks. I've been around hundreds of blocks. Thousands. I know how to do shit, and it's not my fault you don't."

"I know how to do plenty of shit," I say. "And I don't want to stop because I'm pretty sure that cop is waiting for me to get off the highway so he can pull us over."

"Why in the whole wild world would he do that?"

"He doesn't want to get into a high-speed chase with such a fast car."

Yivi clicks her tongue, and I can feel her giving me the look she always gives me before she calls me insane. Which I am, but so is she. "If you legit believe that, then I am genuinely worried about you," she says.

"I believe it."

"Wow!" Yivi shouts before cackling like a cartoon witch because she decided last week that witches have the funniest laughs. "Wowee, wow, wow."

"Shut up."

"But that doesn't make any sense at all, babe."

"It makes sense to me."

"Then you'll be super-duper happy to learn that your incredibly speed-shy cop friend is no longer behind us."

"He isn't?" I ask, before scanning my mirrors and realizing she's right.

"Nope. The coast is clear. And the Cracker Barrel beckons."

"Can you at least wait until we leave Illinois?" I ask, reaching for the Disaronno and guzzling every last drop.

"You're really taking the joy outta this joyride, babe." Yivi fumbles with our booze bag and cracks a warm Miller Lite. "But if it'll make you feel better, I guess I can wait."

"I sincerely appreciate your sacrifice," I say, sighing as the sweet almond liqueur soothes my head and eases my mind. Turns out becoming America's most wanted enby hasn't been awesome for my anxiety. Stealing Clinton's chode-mobile was without a doubt the safest option, but I wish I'd had the keys to a lower-profile vehicle. I was a poor kid, yeah, but not the handy kind. I can't field dress a deer or teach a one-legged rooster to dance, and I sure as shit can't hot-wire a car. My father, on the other hand, can DIY anything. Mr. Fix-It the Union Trim Carpenter. A lifelong disciple of the great and noble blue-collar lifestyle: plunge your own toilet, build your own house, lose your own job. And he lost a shit ton of jobs, man. Weeks of overtime followed by months of unemployment. Not fun for him, and less fun for us. He'd get canned, Mom would flip, and my brother and I would buckle the fuck up, holding our breath until the union office called and the screaming stopped.

My childhood memories are spotty and diffuse, but at some point, in some shimmering display of youthful brilliance, I made it my personal mission to avoid acquiring my father's skills, his opinions, his psychoses, his lot in life. I'll find him if he needs finding, but my going on this trip won't change anything. Because he's like a virus, and I'm fully vaccinated. We do share a few qualities, obviously: the same piggish nose and the same pale skin and the same cosmic dread. But natural stuff—DNA or whatever—that's where our similarities end. I have made damn sure of that.

"The arch!" Yivi shouts, scaring the absolute hell out of me as she pounds the dashboard with her fists. "Is that *the* arch?"

I swish a swig of Jose Cuervo premixed margarita around my mouth and glance out Yivi's window. There it is: the not-so-world-famous Gateway Arch standing sentry at the Illinois-Missouri border. Sleek and silver and mildly impressive if you're an infant child or a wasted twenty-two-year-old garbage goth. "It's smaller than I remember," I say.

"Can we stop?"

"No."

"But we left Illinois."

"Only barely."

"And we need gas."

"This is a heavily populated area."

"But I want to see the motherfucking arch!" Yivi punches my thigh, and I almost swerve into an SUV full of old ladies wearing party hats.

"You just saw it." I massage my stinging quad with my free hand. "That's all there is."

"I don't care. I need real food, and I've gotta pee, and everything's gonna be way worse if we run outta gas on the highway."

"But why would you want to stop *here*?" I ask.

She gives me one of her unfuckwithable looks. "Cuz if you don't . . ." She digs into her fannypack and reveals a gnarly black hunting knife. "I'll gut you head to toe and sell your organs on the black market." She points the knife at my nose. The matte-black blade is six inches long and serrated. Also: very sharp.

"Jesus goddamn Christ, Yivi!" I shout.

"I didn't wanna use this, but you've left me no choice."

I glance between the blade and Yivi's batshit bonkers face to check if she's kidding. All signs point to *probably*, but I can't say for sure. It's been a long time since I was last held at knifepoint, and I don't have fond memories of the experience. My father was never in the military. He certainly never attended boot camp or even took a wilderness-survival course. That, however, did not stop him from forcing my brother and me to train for various end-of-the-world scenarios. I spent the summer before eighth grade learning how to start fires, recycle urine, and escape from restraints. I also learned how to fend off knife-wielding attackers. Too bad I don't remember where you're supposed to hit your assailant on the wrist.

"Fine," I say, checking my mirrors. "Whatever." I veer across three lanes of traffic and onto an off-ramp. "You win."

"Don't get cranky," Yivi says. "It's only a teeny detour."

"I'm not cranky. I'm just not accustomed to being threatened with deadly weapons. And I don't understand why an anti-capitalist revolutionary such as yourself would want to visit a tourist-trappy monument to westward expansion."

Yivi sheathes her knife and places it back into her fannypack. "Cuz a lotta brave racists died so assholes like us could drunk drive our ex-boyfriends' cars wherever we wanted," she says.

"Good point," I say. "Hand me one of those warm Miller Lites."

The Gateway Arch is right off the highway. We pull into a garage and pay a depressed white man sixteen dollars to park. I scan the lot for any sign of cops or cowboys. Yivi sits with her hands folded in her lap while I find a space. She was obviously psyched when I pulled off the highway, but now, she seems oddly nervous. Uncharacteristically quiet. She sleepwalks out of the car, through the garage, and down a drab staircase until we step into the sunlight.

"I've always loved parks," she says, solemnly lifting her gaze to the trees, and I'm surprised. I'd figured her for a hardcore indoor kid thus far, though I guess her basement lifestyle was one of necessity.

"Let's hurry up and get this over with." I stride through the manicured grass, inhaling a mouthful of St. Louis smog. A large crow caws to let us know who's boss, and a mama robin feeds a squirming worm to the world's ugliest baby bird. The pleasures of nature tend to elude me, and today is hot and wet, chokehold humidity despite the high bright sun. The kind of day that reminds me of all the time I spent away from home in childhood, sweating through my oversized Nike shirts and sleeping in my filth on friends' basement floors because I couldn't stand my family.

"Oh, look!" Yivi points a long black fingernail at an obese squirrel perched on a tree stump. "What do you think her li'l name is?"

"Lorie," I say, because it's my mom's name, and my head's too sore for a brainstorm.

Yivi puts her fists on her hips and scrunches up her face. "You can't call a squirrel *Lorie*, babe. That's not even a good name for a person."

"You have a better suggestion?"

Yivi considers this as the squirrel plunges its face into a discarded Fritos bag. "What about Garbage Grace?"

"Works for me."

"Oh shit," Yivi says, her eyes wide. She takes two cartoonishly long steps and ducks behind a weeping cherry tree, hiding within the slender dangling branches. "He's here."

"Who?" I ask, craning my neck to resurvey the park.

"The dude in the tan sedan," Yivi whispers, and I immediately spot an older-model tan Taurus idling on the street near a set of blue porta-potties.

"I thought your dream was about a *truck*," I say, taking cover behind Yivi's tree and peeking through the leaves. There's for sure someone watching us from inside the vehicle, but as far as I can tell, they aren't wearing a cowboy hat.

Yivi cops an attitude: "All I know is it's tan, and that's him."

I chew my cheek, attempting to maintain a healthy skepticism while my heart stampedes toward a panic attack. My father says a lot of very stupid things, but one of his go-to mottos is, *Believe half of what you see and none of what you fear.* Question everything and trust no one. Not even yourself. Or your brand-new BFF Yivi. "You're positive that's Big Gravy's pal?" I ask.

"His *enforcer.*"

It occurs to me that I don't know a whole lot about Big Gravy, and this is too much to process, so I focus on what I do know. "But I've been watching out for a tan truck," I say, fighting to keep my tone as neutral as possible. Lucky for Yivi, a decade spent laboring under capitalism has taught me how to subdue most of my emotions, even amidst a hammering headache. "If I'd been watching for a sedan, I probably would've seen him following us."

"Sorry I'm not an expert in cars."

"You don't need to be an expert to tell a truck from a car," I mutter. At this point, I can't tell if this tan-sedan guy is even looking at us. I also can't decide if he'd be looking at us if we weren't looking at him. "C'mon, Yiv," I say, pulling her back toward the garage. "We'll lose him for real this time."

"Fuck that, babe." She jerks her arm out of my grasp. "I still wanna peep the arch."

"You're kidding."

"Stop stalling and follow me," she says, keeping her head low like a poorly trained army ranger as she makes a run for the tree line.

"If that guy's here because of Big Gravy," I start, "then why hasn't he tried anything?"

"How should I know?" Yivi is walking backward, facing me, and I'm guiding her by the shoulders. Our walking arrangement gives us a 360-degree field of vision so we can stay on the lookout for the tan-sedan guy on our stroll through the park. It also gives Yivi the opportunity to build anticipation as we near the arch. Her brilliant plan is for me to turn her around when we're directly beneath the monument. That way the so-called grandeur can wash over her in its purest form.

"You should know because *you're* the one who worked for Big Gravy," I say.

Yivi wrinkles her nose like she doesn't dig my body odor. "Don't be rude," she says.

"How is that rude?"

"First off, I didn't *work* for him. He was my *partner*. And second, you're assuming that car is following us cuz of me, but it's not like you're some model-citizen-type individual."

"I'm assuming he's following *you* because that's what *you* told me," I say, raising my voice because I'm legitimately spooked. I don't want to admit that I might not be cut out for this life of crime, but I need Yivi to understand that this is not my normal normal.

"It's still a kinda rude assumption," she says.

"I'm on the run from the *cops*, Yivi. Not a crime syndicate."

"Lucky you."

"I'm serious."

"What about Clinton?"

"Who said anything about *him*?"

"Maybe he hired someone else to follow us because you stole his car."

"Clinton's probably not even awake yet."

"Then why are you so worried about cops?" Yivi asks, and I flinch.

I shift my gaze to her cat-head necklace, avoiding her eyes. Call it absurd, but you don't get as far as I did as an unstable fuckup in the corporate world if you don't give yourself rules. No drinking before noon, for example, used to be one of my rules. That's why, when I decided to take this vow of honesty, I also came up with some guidelines. Basically, I can't directly lie, but I *can* hide the truth by omission. When faced with a direct inquiry, however, I am forced to provide an honest response. For the record, I am aware this is completely ridiculous. But I am also aware that telling Yivi I killed my previous best friend might strangle our nascent best-friendship in the cradle. "Because I did something else that was illegal," I say, buying a touch more time.

"No shit, Shakira," Yivi says with a giggle. "But what *kinda* something?"

"It's sort of a long and boring story," I say. "But I . . . I mean . . ."

"You don't gotta tell me right this second if you don't want," Yivi says, and I meet her eyes. Not the biggest or the prettiest or even the brownest, but extremely fucking kind.

"Thank you," I say. "But I promise I'll tell you later."

"Deal."

"Anyway, it's showtime." I steer her sideways until we're perfectly in line with the center of the arch. "Ready?"

Yivi takes a breath. She blinks a bunch of times. "Ready and steady," she says.

I spin her around. She looks up and so do I. The sight isn't super impressive, but I'm rarely wowed by stuff like this. Heroic statues, national monuments, famous hills. I've done my share of great American sightseeing. Road trips and work trips and acid trips in the desert. I've driven past Mount Rushmore, contemplated jumping at Niagara Falls, and bickered with Clinton in Thomas Jefferson's slave dungeon. Last year, I stood at the foot of the Statue of Liberty, feeling nothing except an extremely strong desire to piss into the bay—more out of necessity than a hatred of freedom or whatever. Mostly, I'm burned out on splendor and reverence. Tired of placing my hand over my heart the same way I'm sick of forging time sheets, selling ideas, and flattering clients. There are only so many times you can cry during the national anthem, and my parents joining the Tucker Carlson fan club really took the fun out of watching *The Patriot*.

"Thoughts?" I ask as Yivi's shoulders start to quiver under my palms. I peek around at her face to find her sobbing, mascara coating her cheeks. She pulls away in the direction of the car. I watch her go, then follow. She does this sometimes: loses it. There's a lot going on in her head, I think. More than most people.

"Sorry," she says when I catch up with her.

"It's fine." I make my tone breezy even though I'm actively surveying our general vicinity for villains. "I told you it sucked."

"It didn't suck." Yivi shakes her head, tossing her curls in every direction. "It was cool. Thanks for letting me see it."

"Is he still there?" I ask, peeking through a gap in the low row of hedges dividing this side of the park from the parking garage.

"Nope. All clear."

"You sure?" I check and double-check every single visible vehicle, but it seems she's right. Whoever was spying on us has vanished, and now I honestly don't know if we should be looking out for a car or a truck.

"Positive," Yivi says. "So you can stop being such a wimpy baby bitch about it."

"I'm not being a bitch."

"I was joking."

"Why aren't you worried?"

"What's worry gonna do about it?"

Yivi makes a fair point, and I straighten, massaging my neck where it's sore from endless driving and shitty posture and getting hammered every night for the past fifteen years. I hobble through the parking garage and give the M2 a cursory check for signs of infiltration. Satisfied, I unlock the doors and chug another warm Miller Lite because the Cuervo tastes like Drano.

"Can it be my turn for driving?" Yivi asks—as if I can stop her from doing whatever the fuck she wants.

"I thought you didn't have a driver's license."

"News flash, babe . . ." Yivi leans closer to whisper into my ear. "You don't need a license to drive a stolen car."

Before I can argue, a screeching bird whizzes past my head. It skims the concrete with its wings spread wide before snatching a rodent in its talons.

"Oh no!" Yivi says, grabbing my wrist as the bird zooms out the other side of the parking garage. "Do you think that was Garbage Grace?"

I pop our last beer and slurp warm foam. "Garbage Grace lives outside in the park," I say.

"What if she followed us because she wanted to be friends?"

"Then she was a poor judge of character." I hand Yivi the keys and slide into the passenger seat. I don't like to be driven places because it makes me feel like a child, but my headache is fuzzing my vision, and giving Yivi the wheel means I can grab a nap. My father, on those special nights when he wanted an audience, would often force my family to take rides with him to undisclosed locations. He called them his midnight rides of Paul Revere. We used to ask when we could go home, and he'd say, *When the moon shines bright on Pretty Redwing.* My brother and I never knew what that meant, but we learned not to ask. *Seen and not heard*, my father would say, lashing out with the back of his hand, flattening my already-misshapen nose. In the painful silence that followed, he'd mumble about his latest get-rich-quick idea—real estate tax liens, equine light therapies, memory-boosting fungal elixirs—while Mom stared dead-eyed out the window and ate yogurt-covered pretzels from a Ziploc bag.

Yivi adjusts the driver's seat until her long legs fit comfortably. She grips the wheel at ten and two, then gives me a genuine smile. Her two front teeth are longer than the others, chipmunky and lipstick-smeared, but I'm a big fan.

"You're seriously gonna let me drive?" she asks.

"Why not," I say, closing my eyes and resting my throbbing head against the window. "Just wake me if somebody tries to chop us into sexy little pieces."

The hum of tires over asphalt puts me to sleep for a while. I have a dream that I am God, and my greatest creations are being recalled for factory defects. I stomp over to the assembly line, chew out the angels, and head home to get blitzed and watch old episodes of *Top Chef.* It's not one of the great seasons, but Jenny is among the contestants. I root for her, and she wins the Quickfire Challenge with a fetid pulled-pork casserole. It's very exciting, but instead of celebrating, Jenny shoves her head into a roaring garbage disposal.

I wake up to sirens and flashing lights. "What's happening?" I ask, wiping drool from my chin and remembering I'm not God.

"We might be getting pulled over," Yivi says. "Unless you think I can outrun him?"

I sit up straight and glance over my shoulder. A fat black SUV is waddling up the highway behind us. Another state trooper. I check the speedometer, and we're going almost ninety. Fantastic. I refocus my attention on Yivi. Her sunken cheeks burn with splotches of red, and her eyes glisten with yesterday's mucus. I'm the breed of drinker who can perform sobriety on the verge of collapse, but I'm starting to think Yivi might be a lightweight.

"Whatcha think?" she asks, stomping the accelerator.

"No." I grab the jagged knob of her knee. "Pull over!"

"Don't yell at me."

"I'M NOT GODDAMN YELLING!" I yell.

"This car is hot, babe. We're wasted, and I don't have a license."

"I'm aware," I say. "But this isn't a fucking movie."

"Don't talk to me li—"

"You said a parking lot, Yivi."

"Wha—"

"You said the cops wouldn't pull us over on the *highway*."

"I said they weren't gonna pull *you* over."

"That's a fascinating fucking distinction."

"Dreams ain't exactly a perfect science."

Blood pours past my ears. My throat is dry, and my vision won't focus. A confusing flood of yearning fills me so violently, I think I might drown. I push my fingertips into my eyes. "I need you to pull your shit together and get us out of this."

"Me?" Yivi asks. "Why *me*?"

"Because we . . ." I pause while I prepare to sound incredibly stupid. "Because we need to lie, and I swore on the soul of my dead best friend that I'd only tell the truth from now on."

"What the fuck are you talking about?"

"Just concentrate on what you're gonna say, okay?"

Yivi stares. "Fine." She taps the brake and steers to the side of the road. "But if he shoots us, it's your fault."

"He won't shoot us," I say, though I'm not exactly sure which race box Yivi checks on the census.

Yivi reaches for the Holland House sherry cooking wine, but I beat her to it.

"You're cut off," I say as I toss the bottle into the booze bag and shove the jangling mass under my seat. I roll down my window and burp, wondering how bad we smell. Gravel crunches beneath our tires as we slow, and I switch off the bouncy Doja Cat jam Yivi's been blasting.

The cop stops behind us and sits there a while, probably running our plates. I check the clock, and it's 11:13. If Clinton wanted to go anywhere today, he will have already noticed his car is missing. He's neither a punctual nor overtly litigious person, but there's a chance he's already informed the authorities. This is essentially my nightmare scenario, even if it did not literally appear in Yivi's faulty nightmares.

As I wait for the cop to call for backup, I imagine what my father would say if he knew I was about to be arrested. Our relationship is nontraditional, to say the least. The few times I was suspended from school for breaking windows or lighting fires or telling Mrs. Willis she was a fucking dipshit moron who wasn't qualified to teach spelling, my father greeted me at home like a conquering hero. I don't know what he did, but when he was young, my father got himself kicked out of four different high schools, and he likes to say, *Education exists to manufacture slaves for the ruling classes*. He says, *Respect is earned, not given*. He says, *Fools make rules* and *Cops are the enemy of the people* and, although this is a more recent development, *Blue lives matter.* He is white, old, angry, undereducated, paranoid, and large. He contains multitudes.

"Cops are the worst, man," Yivi says under her breath.

"Real Americans hate cops," I say, fixing my mullet for our mugshots.

After a forever-shaped interval, the cop lumbers out of his car—a big boy, tall and powerful, with wraparound sunglasses and a blonde tuft of beard ruining his chin. The kind of man who enjoys bowling alleys but not bowling. "Good afternoon, miss," he drawls through Yivi's open window. "License and registration."

"I can't find it, sir," Yivi says without hesitation. She heaves each word like a gasp as tears trickle down her face, and her whole body trembles like a Chihuahua in a thunderstorm. Pretty startling performance.

With difficulty, the cop leans down and peers through the open window. Wiry hairs sprout from his nostrils. There's a chunk of something red in his teeth. "What do you mean you *can't find it*?"

I open my mouth to verify her story, but I stop. I know I'm delusional, and I realize that sometimes lying is an act of self-defense, but I made a vow.

"It was an accident, sir," Yivi says, sniffling. She looks up at the cop. "I swear."

"Losing your wallet?"

"And so much money." Yivi drops her forehead onto Clinton's fuzzy red steering wheel cover and commences bawling. "The last thing I'd ever wanna do is break the law," she says between sobs, "but we've gotta get back to St. Louis before somebody takes all my things."

"Is that why you were speeding, miss?" the cop asks, softening his tone. "Because there's no excuse for speeding."

"I'm just *so* sorry." Yivi's chest heaves, and plump little tears plop, plop, plop onto her lap. "I'm such a stupid piece-of-shit idiot,

I could die. I wish you would go ahead and shoot me in my stupid fucking face."

The cop observes me through his sunglasses, and I give him a shrug that says, *At least you don't have to be friends with her.* Frowning, he adjusts his belt buckle and sighs. "Well, I don't know. I suppose I can let you off with a warning if you promise you'll keep things by the book all the way back to St. Louis."

Yivi gasps and lifts her head off the steering wheel. Her cheeks are slick with mascara, her black lipstick is smeared around her mouth, and there's a snot bubble dangling from her nostril. The cop's hand rests on the door, and Yivi places both her palms over his fist. "Thank you, sir. Thank you and thank you and thank you."

"Okay, then, miss." The cop's chin stiffens, and his Adam's apple bobs in his throat. "As long as you promise to drive as safe as you can."

"As safe as I can." Yivi repeats his words like a prayer, and the cop tugs his hand gently from her grasp before returning to his vehicle. I watch him in the rearview as he climbs in, shuts his lights off, and sits there.

"What's he waiting for?" Yivi asks, wiping some excess performance off her cheek.

"Let's go. Drive slow. And take the next exit to make it look like we're heading back."

"I kinda nailed that, didn't I?" Yivi asks, as if we didn't just catch the luckiest break of our lives.

I scowl. "Are you kidding me right now?"

"What?"

"Why the fuck were you driving so fast?!"

Yivi flinches. "Don't yell at me, babe."

"It's just so stupid—"

"And don't fucking call me *stupid*."

"But it *was* stupid, Yiv. You're wasted and reckless, and now you're acting like I'm an asshole for—" I stop lecturing because Yivi's sharp eyes are wet, and her mouth is quivering. For real this time. I guess we haven't reached the point of intimacy where we can scream at each other and get away with it.

"Sorry." I suck a breath and stare out the windshield. I feel like a dick, and now my head is pounding as hard and fast as my pulse. Another drink would help, but this is a fairly hypocritical time to imbibe.

"You *should* be," Yivi says, shifting the car into drive. "Now leave me alone so I can concentrate on the road."

TWO

My father loves to play the unreasonable man. The man who says no when everyone says yes. The man who speaks truth when everyone lies. Tough, crazy, stubborn as hell. In his own confusing way, he fights the power. He flouts norms and marches to the dumb-dumb-dumb of his own wacko drum. He plays dumb with insurance adjusters until they leave him alone. He belittles DMV employees until they let him skip traffic school. He threatens real estate lawyers until they release him from seemingly binding contracts. And I guess I'm supposed to be impressed. My tiny family has long been his sole audience, and he's always found a way to spin his antisocial behavior as a learning opportunity, as if we were all meant to take notes or, at best, become unreasonable assholes ourselves. But I didn't. Couldn't. Partially because I inherited Mom's anxiety, but mostly because I hate being rude. I hate hurting feelings. I'd much rather avoid confrontation. That's the trickiest thing about this radical-honesty stuff. It doesn't necessarily make me mean, but it does make me offensive. Truth, I'm learning, has an odor like vomit. People would prefer you swallow your thoughts or expel them in private. And the constant uncertainty makes it all so much worse. Like, sometimes I say things that feel true, but they don't seem true once I've said them. It's a total mindfuck. Heartfuck. And I want to say some of these things to Yivi, but I don't want to ruin our silence. And I'm worried my thoughts will sound even stupider out loud than they do in my head.

None of what I fear.

None of what I fear.

None of what I fear.

I tilt my head out the open window and let the warm June wind slap my face. I do my best to focus on the not-so-scenic beauty. Missouri is brighter and browner than Illinois, and we're cutting through farm country. Long, bleak rows of sun-bleached crops. Sporadic farmhouses and barns painted white and beige instead of the storybook red that farmers don't seem to bother with anymore. I try to read a billboard about drinking while driving, but I am currently blind in my left eye, and I'll need to drink at least another fifth before I'm fit to drive again. This is the real problem. We are fully fucking dry, but I can't ask Yivi to stop for more booze. I guess I'm afraid she might snap and stab me with her big knife or something. But Yivi would never actually do that. She might be a touch jagged and unpredictable, but she's not violent—and I can tell because I know violent.

I rub the dent in my skull above my left ear. The dent itself isn't sore anymore, but it doesn't feel right. For one thing, it's softer than the rest of my head. For another, it's obviously the source of my headaches. I've endured migraines since puberty, and I'm no stranger to nausea and temporary blindness, but this headache is different. It never completely stops. Tylenol doesn't help, and neither does Excedrin. A frog-faced MinuteClinic doctor back in Chicago assured me the dent was the natural curvature of my skull, but I don't think he liked me enough to tell me the truth. And I know something is off because pressing the dent makes my head hot and loud, like hornets are swarming in the sub-basement of my brain. I do this, now, pushing my thumb into the dent until my left eye unfuzzes. It feels good for a second before my ear starts burning and I nearly puke.

I release the pressure, leaning against the door and breathing through my nose as the blindness returns. It wasn't entirely unexpected: Clinton's outrage the last time we were together. He'd been scary before. Drunk and brutal. In the wet years after college, Clinton had bad moments. Bad days. I never hit back because I'm not that kind of drinker. The only punches I've ever thrown were aimed at my father, and with Clinton, I often felt like I deserved a fist in the face. I would talk trash, start fights, push him too far, comply with my natural programming. And when I finally told him how I truly felt about our relationship, he was in a particularly sensitive mood.

"What're you doing?" I hazard to ask when Yivi flips on the turn signal and swerves toward an exit.

"I saw a sign for some shopping," she says without looking at me. "And I'm worried you're gonna die if I don't get you something to drink."

"I'm probably not going to die," I say, though I'm touched she cares enough to consider my health.

"Either way, we need a refill."

"Good call," I say. "And I really am sorry about—"

"I don't wanna talk about it," Yivi says. "But if you ever yell at me like that again, we're not friends anymore."

Yivi tells me to watch the car while she runs into a Walmart Supercenter for Birthday Cake ingredients, and I don't argue. I couldn't shop right now, even if I wanted. I can't do much but sit here and wait until my sight returns. One thing I especially cannot do is talk to my mom, but after two and a half seconds of relative peace and quiet, my fucking iPhone begins to ring.

"I've got a major headache, so I can't talk long," I say by way of greeting.

"Are you coming or not?" Mom asks, charming as ever.

"Of course I'm coming," I say, though if it weren't for a certain cowboy guy, I'd still be face-down on my futon.

"There's no reason to take that tone," Mom says. "It's not *my* fault that I figured you'd blow me off like usual."

"I don't blow you off," I say, and it's mostly true. I've been avoiding a lot of her calls lately, but I answered last night, and we usually talk like once a month. I even sent her a gift card to Massage Envy on her birthday. We aren't exactly cool, but my problems with Mom are much subtler than my problems with my father. In fact, most are in the form of questions: *Why'd you follow him to Arkansas? Why'd you stay married for fifty years? Why didn't you protect us?* One might think a psychotherapist could provide me some nifty and productive answers to these questions, but I have spent enough time in therapy to say with some certainty that no, nuh-uh, they cannot.

"How're you getting down here?" Mom asks.

"I stole Clinton's car."

"That's nice of him to lend it to you."

I roll my eyes. "Do you know where Henry went?" I ask.

"He's nutso again," she says. "Just more of his freaky woo-woo bullshit."

"I assumed that much." *Woo-woo bullshit* is the catch-all term Mom uses for my father's odd obsessions and conspiracy theories. Past-life regression, colloidal silver treatments, the spiritual path of Eckankar, and MedBed investment schemes would fall into the category of odd obsessions. The melting temperature of steel beams, the HAARP weather-control center, the Bilderberg reptiles, the illegitimacy of mail-in ballots, and the Global Plandemic occupy the latter category. "But where is he?" I ask.

"I already told you I don't know," she says, her voice rising.

"I guess I forgot."

"You sound terrible."

"It's just this headache."

"Probably a hangover."

"When'd he leave?"

"How long till you get here?"

"I don't know, Mom. I asked you a question."

"He's been gone for over two weeks. And his phone's disconnected."

"TWO *WEEKS*?!" I ask, louder than intended, and the vibration of my own voice sends a fiery jolt of pain to the base of my skull. I take a breath and soften my tone. "Why didn't you call me sooner?"

"I've been calling you every single day," she says.

I massage the spongy spot in my skull. It's possible she's exaggerating, but it's also possible I ignored all her calls. "What about the cops or whatever?" I ask.

"The Hookville Sheriff's Office told me they don't deal with domestic issues."

"And you want me to kidnap him?"

"I just need you to help me find him and bring him home," she says, as if I am the one who married an overgrown toddler. "Now, please tell me when you're planning on getting here so I can sort out dinner."

"Soon," I say. "Tonight."

"Are they giving you time off work?" she asks. "I know how those people get when you try to take a vacation. Poor Jenny acts like she'll die without you around."

I cringe. The last thing I want to do is chat about Jenny, and the primary benefit of avoiding Mom's calls is I haven't updated her on my recent life changes. "They don't need me in the office right now," I say.

"What do you mean?"

"I mean they fired me. And also I quit."

Mom is quiet for a stretch. "What?"

"I'll give you the backstory when I see you," I say, and I hang up before she can reply. My head is throbbing harder than ever, and the guilt I feel in letting that aging woman down is surprisingly immense. An absurd reaction. Because this, all of this, is at least partially her fault. My father might be the broken brain behind my broken life, but she is the broken heart.

Several long minutes pass. Mom calls a few more times before I shut off my phone. The air-conditioning soothes my face, and I recline my chair. I give the parking lot one last cursory check for cops and cowboys, hoping I still have time to grab a nap before Yivi emerges.

Too late. I blink to unfuzz my vision, and yeah, Yivi has already left the store. She's strutting toward the car with her arachnid arms spread wide and giant Walmart bags hanging from each hand. The afternoon sun is glowering, glinting off her grease-soaked black curls. Long vibrating lines of heat rise from the parking lot pavement, and Yivi moves her hips like a strung-out feature rapper in a Cardi B video. It's music to my soul, and for a moment, I almost forget that my life is entirely fucked. Then I realize Yivi isn't alone.

I stagger from the car as Yivi and a stranger, possibly a very old white lady, approach. The midday heat sends my blood up immediately, and I pant. A fire rages from my amygdala to my toes. Cars rattle, trucks moan, children argue, and above it all, Yivi cackles like a witch. Normally, this sound brings me mild-to-moderate joy, but here among the nauseating stench of a Subway-sandwich breeze, Yivi's goofy laughter sounds mocking and weird, like a banshee's hateful screech. I cover my ears, trying instead to focus my good eye on the bloated promise of Yivi's grocery bags. Surely, these bags are packed with a clear overabundance of liquor that Yivi has purchased with my debit card, a card I gave her free rein to use and abuse because wasting money, for me, is better than therapy.

Mom raised me to fear poverty more than death, but over the course of my relatively successful professional career, I have managed to throw away my meager wealth as often as possible, if only to prove I can. I love spending hundreds of dollars on sushi dinners, letting SSENSE packages sit unopened in my closet, and paying for Yivi's rent and her food and whatever other nonsense she asks for. A fat salary was my only American dream growing up. I long thought—or maybe hoped—that my family's problems stemmed more from poverty than inherent dysfunction. This hypothesis has since been thoroughly nullified, but watching money leave my bank account still gives me a semi-erotic jolt. I may no longer be gainfully employed, but I made enough in my twenties to lay an ugly little nest egg. Last I checked, I still had around 100K in checking, so Yivi and I can keep living like gutter queens for a while longer before I'll need to wash my hair and land another job—provided she doesn't do something stupid like offer a ride to an elderly narc.

"Yo, yo, baby-o," Yivi says as she reaches the car, and the very old white lady turns out to be a fairly young white girl with rampant acne and grayish pigtails and huge, bulging eyes.

"Hello, Yivi," I say. "Who's this?"

"I thought you said your name was Tai," the girl says, and Yivi gives me a wink.

"Yivi is one of my many nicknames," she says before gesturing to the ugly white girl. "And this is Becky."

I suppress a grimace. If Yivi needs to use aliases to elude her various stalkers, then she should probably stop making new friends. "Weird to meet you, Becky," I say.

"Becky works the checkout at Walmart," Yivi says. "And I sorta made a dealski with her in exchange for some free drinks."

"But we didn't need a deal, Yivi," I say, forcing a smile to prevent my mouth from descending into fury.

"Clearly," Becky says, and I follow the greed of her gaze to our stolen M2.

"A penny saved is a penny made, babe."

I smile wider, hoping my mouth is approaching a Jack Nicholson level of mania, and aim my face at young Becky. In a more ideal world, merely witnessing such an expression on the puffy face of a dirty, rotten burnout like myself would scare this girl back into the depths of the Walmart from whence she came. Unfortunately, young Becky seems brave. She returns my smile, and I realize that, despite her pimply cheeks, stringy hair, and cartoonish eyes, she is actually quite a nice-looking person. "That is such a great point, Yivi," I say.

"How long have you two been married, by the way?" Becky asks, for some reason.

"We've been together five years," Yivi says before I can interject. "Just like you and your boyfriend."

"My boyfriend works at the Motel 6 up the road," Becky says, as if this snippet of info explains something about anything.

Yivi hands me one of the grocery bags, and the weight nearly knocks me off-balance. "Me and Becky got to talking," she says. "And when I found out she had a hookup at the motel, we decided it'd be fun to have a party."

Becky leans closer and whispers what must be a secret: "I pretended to check Tai out, but we kinda stole all this stuff."

"Becky likes to drink, but she's only seventeen," Yivi adds.

"Fabulous," I say, and I stop grinning. My jaw aches. The Walmart logo bothering my right eye flickers in and out of view. I haven't been fully blind since the actual moment that Clinton smacked me upside the head with his White Sox 2005 World Series commemorative baseball bat, but now, as I struggle to maintain consciousness, I feel an odd nostalgia for the initial pain of my head injury. There was a sharp and startling clarity in those sensations. As I stumbled into Clinton's elevator and through the lobby and down the South Loop streets, I felt free. I felt as if everything I had been or done was leaking out, borne by blood, through the fissure in my scalp. The rest of that day is hazy, but I remember thinking the pain was a lot like happiness. I also remember the pain was not like now. At the risk of sounding alarmist, I think I might be dying. I think Yivi's completely unnecessary decision to break one more bullshit law might be the last rusty nail that seals my curious coffin. I have always harbored the common fear of the common queer—the deep, dark anxiety that either my gender identity or my Pornhub search history might one day land me in prison—but it goes without saying that my father is the only unreasonable lawbreaker in my family. When I was younger, before I ever learned to fear the innately illicit nature of my own existence, I used to worry my father's schemes would eventually get the whole bunch of us thrown in jail. Forgery scams and tax evasions, unethical Costco returns and complicated plots to exceed the per-customer limit on two-for-one McMuffins. One time, a strapping young Comcast dude came to our door and accused us of stealing cable. A few months prior, I'd sweated away an afternoon holding a ladder while my father snatched the Comcast filter off the telephone pole behind our house. I figured the jig was up, but my father went Adam-Sandler-nuclear, red-faced and hollering that the tech should be fired for harassment. It was excruciatingly embarrassing watching him chase that Comcast guy all the way back to his truck, and I try to avoid putting myself into those kinds of situations now that I can afford to live inside the lines of the law. And yet here I am. A thief. A murderer. An accessory to underage indulgence. And it's essentially my own doing. I could also blame Clinton or Jenny or Yivi or, yeah, my whole entire family, but in the end, fault is irrelevant. I am officially blind, sick, fading, and fully at the mercy of my garbage-goth companion. I could scream or throw a fit in front of this Becky girl. I could tell Yivi I don't need her friendship. I could say a lot of things that aren't based in reality. The truth, however, is that I cannot currently get myself to Arkansas without Yivi's help. I need her like Republicans need trans folks in a post-Dobbs world. And I might need a drink even more.

"You okay, babe?" Yivi asks as I spin a slow pirouette and hobble blindly back to the car.

"I'm excellent, Tai," I say. "Let's get this shitshow back on the road."

"Heyyy, my love," Becky chirps, as I follow the sound of her voice and the thumpity-thump of Yivi's Doc Martens into the Motel 6. I mean, I'm not 100 percent echolocating. I can see the void of Yivi's black tights and the tasteless blur of young Becky's oversized jeans. Beyond that, I can make out the shape of blue walls, uncomfortable neo-modern chairs, and the free-stale-coffee urns that make the lobby of any Motel 6 so warm and welcoming. I can also infer based on the gypsum-dust odor that, past the lobby, the elevator bank is a construction zone with bare drywall and plastic sheets protecting the carpet. I pinch my nose to stanch a trauma sneeze. Unable to properly exorcise his carpentry demons due to his chronic unemployment, my father used his spare energy to compulsively undertake renovation projects he rarely finished. As such, our entire house was a semidemolished construction site. The bedroom I shared with my brother was gutted and drafty, crammed with toolboxes, half-full paint cans, spare lumber, random buckets of jagged hardware, and other child-friendly health hazards. The only upside was all that crap gave me plenty of hidey-holes for Ice Mountain bottles filled with vodka by the time I got to seventh grade.

"Becky! My dear! What brings you to the 6?" asks the presumably teenaged clerk behind the fake-marble counter.

"Dipped outta work early so we could have a party," Becky says. "And I brought some new friends."

"Charmed to meet you," the clerk says, and while I cannot quite perceive features on his pink smudge of a head, I can definitely tell that his haughty manner of speech does not match the reedy, wavering timbre of his voice.

Yivi hoists her Walmart bags above the counter. "Your girlfriend said you'd hook us up with a room if we shared some of this tasty liquor."

The clerk pushes what seems to be a long swoop of bangs out of his face, and I briefly wonder how much My Chemical Romance has trickled down to his generation. "You must mean my *fiancée*," he says.

"I didn't realize y'all were engaged," Yivi says, as if she is genuinely excited for them.

"Aren't you both a little young for marriage?" I ask.

"True love is a once-in-a-lifetime opportunity, sir," the clerk says, assuming my gender as he simultaneously assumes that I'm interested in his perspective. "My birth parents didn't understand that fact," he continues, "and they're dead now."

"Oh no," Yivi says. "I'm so sorry to hear that."

"Don't be." The clerk glances at what I assume is a janky Lenovo monitor. "They made their choices." He puckers his purplish lips. "And I'll just need your names for the reservation."

"I'm Tai. Tai Gunderson," Yivi says, using my surname, and I flinch as she points a sharp black thumbnail at me. "And this one is currently nameless."

"You don't have a name?" Becky asks.

Her fiancé tugs at the not-quite-chin-shaped bottom of his blobby face. "Most people possess names," he says.

"I recently abandoned it," I say.

"Are you transgender?" Becky asks, not unkindly, and I've gotta hand it to her, it's a remarkably perceptive and liberal question for this part of the country. Maybe I'm starting to look a bit less binary these days. Or maybe Becky came of age in a more enlightened decade. I wonder what Jenny would say.

"Who knows what I am." I wave away the seriousness of

Becky's inquiry. "Y'all can just check me in under Fuckhead if it makes things easier."

Becky presses her fist over her lips to stifle what she must consider an inappropriate laugh. "I don't think he can check you in under that, but I get where you're coming from. I have a really good friend who's transitioning, and their mom's been a totally massive jerk about it."

"Most people suck," Yivi says.

"That is not necessarily true," the clerk says.

"Can we do this faster?" I ask. "I'd love to lie down."

"Um, alright . . . I suppose I can make an exception . . ." The clerk clicks around on his keyboard. "Do either of you have any identification?"

"What if you just gave us a key card since we're mainly here for a party?" Yivi asks.

"Yeah, Dante," Becky says. "Just give them the Underwater Honeymoon Suite."

The clerk also known as Dante seems to consider this. "That would be highly unorthodox," he says.

Yivi plops an elbow on the counter, and her already-extraordinary charm increases exponentially. "So is having a party with two fun dummies you just met," she says. "But all the best things in life are pretty unorthodox."

"Just give us the room," I say, because, like Yivi's charm, my resignation seems to be doubling with every passing second. I would drop dead right here in this lobby, but after fending off the specter of suicide for so many years, it feels wrong to die in motherfucking Missouri.

"I really and truly would," Dante says. "Unfortunately, the Underwater Honeymoon Suite is especially reserved for lovers like my darling Becky and I."

"You two are married, though, right?" Becky asks.

"We're crazy in love," Yivi says, leaning her head on my shoulder. "Think of us like Romeo and Juliet but with a couple more problems."

"Hark, thy roometh needeth a security checketh," Yivi says, striding across the Underwater Honeymoon Suite and peering through the big plate glass window. She opens the curtains and surveils the parking lot while I take a predominantly olfactory tour of the room's supposedly deep-ocean experience. To say the various odors hit my nose like a wave would be both too clever and too kind—old Band-Aids, dirty thongs, cigarette filters, a touch of lemon. I won't pretend it smells worse than the Cleveland Marriott where I brought Jenny the drugs that ended her life, but the scent here is certainly more organic. It's a good thing Dante and Becky said they'd hang downstairs while Yivi and I got settled. I wouldn't want to offend them when I compulsively inspect this mattress and read the bedbugs like braille.

"Valorous news!" Yivi says, thrusting her fannypack into the air with both hands. "Yonder parking lot doth show no scant trace of coppers or tan-colored carriages."

I toss my phone, keys, and wallet onto what I think is an oddly shaped nightstand and lurch over to Yivi. She has been talking like discount Shakespeare since we left the lobby, and I have officially reached the end of my fuse. "Give me the fucking booze, Guildenstern," I say.

"There beeth no needeth to sweareth, my babeth."

I snatch one of the bags from her hand, and the plastic tears, spilling six bottles of brown liquor and a sack of green blobs onto the carpet, but nothing else. "What the hell is this?" I ask.

"Do ye not loveth thee olde Captain of Morgan?"

"I fucking asked you to get vodka and shit."

Yivi witch cackles, throwing back her head. "Oh my Todd, *chill*," she says, invoking the fuckboy deity we made up because Yivi says only an asshole named Todd could have created a universe this shitty.

I grab the other bag from Yivi and peek inside to find six warm bottles of Coca-Cola. "What about Birthday Cakes?" I ask.

"I'm in a Cuba libres kinda mood."

I grind my molars in the direction of the offensive liquor. The depressing cola. Jenny's favorites. I swallow. I try not to scream. Yivi doesn't know anything about Jenny, and she definitely doesn't know Jenny used to call rum and Cokes *Cheapo Cruisers*. We would make them at her desk when we were working late without cocaine. They burn cleaner than most cocktails, and they keep you going. Jenny was a few years older than me, and she had a very Paris Hilton sense of humor. Her North Dakota childhood and University of Illinois education made her a skosh more basic than most of my other friends. She used to mix our drinks in these massive pink wineglasses she kept in her desk. The glasses said BETCH #1 and BETCH #2, and I don't know why, but she always insisted I be first betch. "Whatever," I say, snatching a bottle of Captain off the floor and retreating into the bathroom.

"Where you headed, babe?"

"I need a minute."

"Are you okay?"

"I have never been okay."

"Do you wanna talk about it?"

I shake my head because I'm way too tired to waste my breath. And I've already wasted plenty. To psychiatrists and social workers, to Jenny and Clinton, to mentors and professors

I don't talk to anymore. At this point, it's all just rancid mind gunk, angsty pubes caught in the shower drain of my brain.

"You sure?" Yivi asks.

"I'll be out in a bit." I lock the bathroom door and fumble for a light switch. When I find one, the dark gray blur turns dark blue. For all its flaws, the Airbnb back in Chicago featured a pretty solid shower, and I've found that, while getting massively drunk is the optimal cure, a torrent of scalding water seems to help with my headaches as well. Plus, I stink, and if I go permanently blind, I'll need to start taking my various body odors a lot more seriously.

I shuffle across the tiles and crank on the shower. Heat screams out from the head. I peel off my stank-rich Fear of God T-shirt, my annihilated Versace socks, my festering Beams Plus jeans. A steamy cloud clings to my face as I futz with the rum bottle. My nasty nails could use a trim, but they make it easy to tear the plastic off the cap. I twist the top, climb into the tub, and open my throat.

The Captain Morgan tastes better than I remembered. Sweet, spicy, and a lot like high school. Jenny preferred Mount Gay, which really was an excellent choice. She used to shout, *Let's get gay!* when we were alone at the office. We would run the halls and trash the kitchens, and yeah, when things got weird, we fucked in some meeting rooms. She was my advertising art director, my ride or die, my best friend. I would watch her work after all my copy was written. She'd design our presentations, and I'd sit behind her with my feet propped on her desk, reclining in my Herman Miller with a Cheapo Cruiser in my lap. The closest thing I've ever had to a happy place.

It wasn't exactly *Mad Men*, but we got shit done. We won awards, clients, and the minds of millions of idiots we convinced to sign up for credit cards. Sometimes we sold nice things like skincare or streaming services, but normally it was poisonous foods and drinks and debt. If I sound anything like proud of that, let me be extra clear that I'm not. I've never had much use for my career beyond its capacity to improve my financial station. I have written coherent screenplays and competent manuscripts and semi-tasteful poetry, but nobody ever paid me for that garbage. Nobody flew me to California to eat free Michelin-starred sushi and shoot with Spike Lee because I had real artistic merit. They did it because I could sell hard, talk smart, and make dipshit tasteless clients feel like their opinions mattered. Together, Jenny and I were unstoppable. We were sick, drunk, and stressed, but we also had one-way tickets to the kinds of jobs that allow lower-middle-class kids to pretend we might one day join Bezos on Mars. We were lying to ourselves and each other, enabling our mutual habits and delusions, and there were days when we might have been in love. Without Jenny, I feel subhuman. Not a man or a queer but a creature. Yivi has played the part of a halfway decent partner in crime, but I'd always hoped to share a nursing home with Jenny St. Marsh. A morphine drip with a pair of IV lines. Two poor, angry fools who made something like good.

"Hey, babe?" Yivi asks, rapping "Shave and a Haircut" on the bathroom door and interrupting my downpour of self-pity.

The shower has finished removing my top layer of face, and I wipe water from my eyes. My vision seems to be returning, which bodes well. I can now see that the showerhead is a whale tail, the shower curtain is a deep-blue gradient, and the bar soap is a sea turtle. Beneath my toes, the floor of the tub resembles waves, and the wall tiles are inset with decorative fish shapes. For a Motel 6, the effect is almost tasteful. For any other hotel, the effect is suburban mom with an eight-hundred-dollar gift card to Hobby Lobby. "What's up?" I say as I stop the shower.

"You've kinda been in there a while."

"Not long enough."

"You're also getting, like, billions of texts from Clinton."

My bottle of Captain sloshes in the bathroom silence as I take another drink. While I would prefer that Yivi didn't read my private messages, I'm not mad she is using my phone. She microwaved hers to prevent anyone from tracking her, but she still likes to check TikTok occasionally to make sure the MAGA fascists haven't started their purges. And I get that. "What's he saying?" I ask, once my whistle feels wet enough to continue our conversation.

"He said, *Did you take my car?*"

"A tremendously deductive question."

"He also says he loves you, and he's worried, and he isn't mad because he just wants you to come home."

"Classic manipulation tactics."

"What should I say?"

I throw a scratchy blue bathrobe over my shoulders and step out of the tub. Literally everything in this bathroom is blue, from the seashell toilet seat to the fish-mouth faucet, and while I enjoy this particular color as much as the next depressed person, it's honestly a bit much. "Tell him to go fuck his father," I say.

Yivi doesn't respond right away. Eventually, she asks, "What's your deal, babe?"

"I really did not want to come to this motel, Yivi."

"But I thought you liked parties."

"You knew bringing your Walmart girl to the car would strong-arm me into doing whatever you wanted."

"I don't see what the big deal—"

"PEOPLE ARE CHASING US!" I shout, and a full-body rage spasm slops what's left of the rum onto my robe.

"Don't yell at me."

"I can't help it! You are driving me crazy! We are running from cops! We are hiding from Big Gravy! And my fucking father—who I *fully* fucking hate—has been missing for two whole weeks!"

Yivi is silent for another awkward interval. When she finally speaks, I can barely hear her through the door. "How the heck was I supposed to know that?" she asks.

"I didn't realize I needed to keep you abreast of every little update."

"You know what, babe? I get that you're stressed, but you're also being a total fucking asshole—and I was already having second thoughts about Arkansas."

"What do you mean?" I ask, though I have an idea. There's a metric Trumpton of factors, but the Arkansas move was the straw that shattered the already-pretty-broken camel's back of my relationship with my father. Arkansas was his idea, his plan, his mission. He dragged Mom south, and since they left Illinois, their mutual worldviews haven't exactly improved. It might be stupid to blame a state for their state of mind, but I'm too exhausted to differentiate causality from correlation. If I were Yivi, and I had a choice, I wouldn't want to face the country music either.

"I mean I only wanna go on this freaky trip if you promise to stop being so rude," Yivi says.

"I'm only being rude because you're being childish."

Yivi makes a sound that is somewhere between a grunt, a groan, and a scream.

"Case in point," I say.

"I swear I shoulda stayed in Chicago."

I'm not sure what I can say that won't escalate this little spat, so I squeegee the mirror with the sleeve of my robe. The vision in my left eye is still pretty fuzzy, but the iris looks almost normal. Shiny and tired and the same color blue as the countertop. I contort my mouth into a sultrier shape and push my bangs off my forehead. I normally avoid my reflection these days, but I might as well get a good look before I see Mom and my self-esteem turns to ash. Aside from my stupid haircut, I look pretty tolerable. Not as rotten as I feel. My cheeks are splotchy and raw, my stubble's getting stubblier, and I'm probably dying of liver disease, but I've still got the majority of my beauty. My natural symmetries. My Sydney Sweeney lips. Even with these ultrabright vanity lights, it's hard to see the subtle crater Clinton bashed into my skull, and my upturned nose looks less piggish than usual. With fresh clothes and the right Korean skincare products, I could probably pull myself out of this tailspin. I'll just need to kick my copilot out of the plane. "Yeah," I say when I can no longer contain myself, "maybe you should have."

"What's that, Miss Mumbles?" Yivi asks.

"MAYBE YOU SHOULD HAVE!"

"Oh. Yeah. Right." Yivi cackles, less like a witch and more like a rude-ass chick who thinks I'm pathetic. "You're crazy if you think you can do this shit solo."

"I can."

"No, babe. You *can't*."

"Why not?"

"You clearly just can't."

"This is an incredibly juvenile argument, Yivi."

"I totally agree—and it's because *you're* being an incredibly juvenile asshole. Exhibit A: You're pouting in the bathroom instead of having a drink with me. And if you seriously wanna know why I decided to slow this shit down, it's because I think you're kinda losing it. You're freaking out, and you're acting crazy, and you're paranoid as fuck."

"I'm not the one dreaming of cowboys."

"Excuse me for using my Todd-given gift of sight to keep you safe."

"If this is *safety*, I really do not want to experience *danger*."

"You're the one running from the cops for some mysterious reason."

"Don't make fun of my shit."

"Stop being so fucking sensitive."

"I would like to leave this dump immediately, Yivi."

"I know, I know," she says, and I can almost hear her fidgeting with her cat-head necklace. "But I made you a Cuba libre," she continues, "and the Coke is already getting flat."

I shake my head at myself in the mirror. "Fine." I open the door to find Yivi wearing a bathrobe identical to mine. She raises a bleached eyebrow at the voided rum bottle in my hand. "It better be as good as a Birthday Cake," I say.

"Obviously," she says, handing me the drink. "Now tell me who you killed."

I nearly choke tasting the Cheapo Cruiser. Instead, I manage to swallow half before removing it from my lips. It tastes better than I'd expected with such shitty rum. "What the fuck's that supposed to mean?" I ask.

"It's just an expression."

"I don't think it is." I slide past Yivi and float across our suite. The décor out here is far more atrocious than the bathroom.

Mismatched, garish, kitschy. The nightstands are purple and shiny. The king-sized bed is a giant pink seashell. The TV sits atop a pirate's treasure chest, and there's a very odd yellow sofa that looks specifically designed for gymnastic intercourse. Even if the walls weren't completely covered with fake maritime oil paintings, it would still be the ugliest room in America.

"But for real, babe," Yivi says, "if you wanna keep these good times rollin', you need to tell me why you're so scared of the police."

I toss my empty bottle into a trash can under the minibar. Bits of mutilated lime rind lie like shrapnel on the counter. Yivi must have used her teeth to tear apart the garnish for our cocktails. I stiffen my drink with another couple shots of Captain and turn back to her. "It's really none of your business," I say.

"It *is* since you made me your partner in crime," Yivi says, taking a seat on the edge of the seashell bed. She sips her beverage, and the look she gives me over the rim of her glass makes it clear that I'm not about to talk her out of storytime.

"That's why you're better off not knowing," I say.

Yivi scrutinizes me with a frown. "You're, like, legit scared about this, aren't you?"

"Som—" I start, but before I can explain, there's a knock on the door.

"Oh shit, oh shit." Yivi straightens on the bed. "Guess it's party o'clock."

"You sure that's the kids?" I stare at the doorknob, listening for voices, but the only thing I can hear is the Coke fizzing in our glasses.

"Their names are Dante and Becky."

"I know their names." I tighten my bathrobe belt. "But you need to help me get rid of them, okay?"

"I could do that," Yivi says with a shimmering shittiness in her eyes. "But only if you tell me what you did."

"I'll tell you as soon as we're back in the car."

"What about your truth-vow thingy?"

"What about it?"

"I'm asking you to be *honest*, and you're not doing it."

I open my mouth, but before I can mount a compelling defense, I'm interrupted by a louder knock at the door. I flinch each time the knuckles strike wood. "Hello?" calls a voice that does, indeed, sound like Becky's. "Are y'all decent?"

"One sec," I shout. "We're coming." I turn back to Yivi. "Can we *please* just tell them we're leaving?"

Without a word, Yivi stands and sashays across the carpet. I say her name three times before she reaches the door. I consider chasing her, grabbing her arm and demanding confirmation, but I'm positive she's not going to cooperate. And I'm also positive that she's almost as infuriating as I am.

THREE

My father is not a people person. He hates crowds and loathes pleasantries. His interpersonal policies have always been isolationist, and whether he did so by choice or by habit, he succeeded in cutting my family off from the outside world. My brother and I learned early on not to invite other kids over to our place, and Mom was never allowed to have anything resembling a social life. Any friends she made were classified as snooty bitches or dipshit dirtbags. He called her side of the family *the Hillbillies*, and his side were just *the Fucks*. As a result, we didn't see my cousins much. I can barely remember my aunts' and uncles' names. Mom fought to keep her mother in our life, but my father's own mother wasn't allowed around. I didn't see Grandmama Gunderson for over ten years before she passed, and I didn't find out she'd died of cancer until a collection agent called to pressure my father into paying her outstanding medical bills.

I don't know too many concrete details about his childhood, so I can't speak to any specific traumas that might have made my father antisocial, but I think it might be a Gunderson family trait. I am certainly a tad judgmental by nature. I find most people ignorant, ugly, tasteless, pathetic, unfashionable, dirty, and generally offensive, but I still make a daring attempt to tolerate the human animal. Jenny wasn't perfect, but she was the one I'd chosen, my first step in becoming a socialite who could have and keep real friends. With her gone, a large part of me believes I'm destined to die young and alone, but a smaller part, the part that wants to live, hopes I've got time to start over.

Somehow, by some miracle, Yivi can stand me. I am at my worst, my lowest, my drunkest, but she's still here. If I wanted to steer into my genetic slide, I'd simply throw on my clothes, grab a couple bottles of Captain, and race out of this shithole town. Instead, for better or probably worse, I am going to try and leave this dump with Yivi by my side.

"Under the sea!" Becky sings, shimmying into the room.

I lurch sideways to give her an unobstructed path to the bed, and she Supermans onto the comforter. Dante watches like a proud parent as she faceplants. My mind sprints circles, and I kill the remainder of my drink. I try to make eye contact with Yivi. I wish I had the guts to tell her about Jenny. She is standing by the door, frowning slightly with a faraway look that obscures her thoughts. I raise my brow, but she won't give me her attention, like I've ceased to exist.

"I hope you two lovers are enjoying your stay so far," Dante says as he strides into the room carrying two grease-spotted sacks of Popeyes. "I see you have already taken advantage of the Wild Wave Shower Experience."

"Yep," I say, and now that I can appraise them more clearly, I give Dante and Becky a primal once-over and conclude neither could ever be my type. Too scrawny, slouchy, limp. Soft-chinned youngs destined to grow into soft-bellied olds. Not nearly as strapping as me at their age, with my addiction to *Men's*

Health workouts and my varsity soccer thighs. Growing up with an overweight pig-nosed father—and a mom who called him *empty belly* and *porko* and *fat piece of shit* when they weren't even fighting—gave me a very special relationship with my body. It's probably unfair that I judge others based on my own self-hatred, but I can't help it. Plus, it's fun.

"This is my favorite room in the whole world," Becky says, and somehow, her big, bulging eyes manage to increase in size. "It's just like being in the ocean."

"It even smells like fish," I say. "But unfortunately, we've had a change of plans."

"What kinda change?" Becky asks.

"We need to get back on the road sooner than we thought, so we might not have time for a party."

"There's always time for a party, babe," Yivi says, and I realize she's slipped behind me, making a stealthy beeline for the minibar. I can feel Dante studying my damp hair and raw face. I lift my drink and remember I'm empty.

"No, Yivi. There *isn't*," I say with a bit more force. "We're in a hurry, remember?"

"Bummer," Becky says. "I was pretty excited to hang."

"Don't listen to Sergeant Sourpuss over there," Yivi says.

"But my mom is expecting us tonight," I say, and I squeeze my cup in both hands. If the glass shattered and the shards slashed my palms, I could probably convince these kids that I needed medical attention. I wouldn't mind the pain, but it would be risky to go to a hospital, and it's not an awesome idea to drive six more hours with deep and unstitched wounds.

"Is that really *true* though, babe?" Yivi says, and even if she hadn't said the word *true* like a taunt, I'd still know I was being mocked.

"Of course it is."

"Either way, you're too drunk to drive."

"I'm not the one who's going to be driving."

"Neither am I," Yivi says with an infuriating grin. "And I guess that settles it."

I focus all my energy into a rageful glare, but her grin only gets shittier. I like Yivi, I really do, but I hate being fucked with. As a slight, soccer-playing, not-super-masc-type child, I usually arrived home from school with my books caked in mud. Teachers teased me, friends taunted me, jocks pushed me around. My soft, smoochable face has always lacked the pugnacity to intimidate, and while I start most days with a series of hangover-curing calisthenics, no number of push-ups will ever build my body into that of a cage fighter. Some people, including my father, can frighten others through sheer craziness, but unlike misanthropy, his ferocity must have skipped a generation. As such, I am an alpha in the body of a beta. A leader with the voice of a follower. A highly skilled professional with the posture of a heroin addict. Clinton was my top, my father was my chieftain, and despite Jenny's charming insistence, I was always betch #2. With Yivi, though, I refuse to resign myself to the sidecar. She thinks I'm a pushover, a joke, a dunce she can lead around by the nose, but she's about to learn I've got more than eczema up the sleeves of this scratchy-ass bathrobe.

Yivi and I take the seashell chairs, and the kids cuddle on the yellow fuck sofa. Dante unloads his Popeyes sacks onto the hideous coffee table occupying the center of our sitting area. The surface of the table is glass, a tri-hue swirl of blue, not dissimilar to a toilet when you flush some bowl cleaner, and each of Dante's cardboard food containers looks like a turd circling the drain. As Dante works, Becky rambles on about Walmart, and Yivi sips a fresh cocktail from her shiny blue glass. I, on the other hand, have abandoned my glassware. Kissing the cold, hard mouth of the Captain bottle reminds me of Clinton whenever I swig, and chugging this rum straight from the bottle is part of my strategy to spook these kids into cutting short Yivi's evening.

"It's honestly crazy," Becky continues. "Like, I've always wondered what would happen if I just took some stuff I wanted at work, but I never thought I'd really do it."

"It's liberating, though, right?" Yivi asks.

Dante unseals the last of his battered Popeyes boxes, and the stench that emerges is less hot chicken than warm carcass. "It was also quite risky," he says.

"But it takes a risky to win the bisky!" Yivi says, snatching a biscuit off the table.

Becky giggles, and I seize my chance. I burp and lurch forward. "It was also extremely fucking dumb," I say, slurring my words to appear far drunker than I actually am.

Becky's bulging eyes pulse, and Dante glances up from his food. They both look at Yivi, then back at me. I wrap my lips around my bottle, deliberately allowing a trickle of rum to escape from the corner of my mouth, and all at once, I'm filled with the icy-hot rush of joyful exhilaration. Until now, speaking my mind has felt like a burden. But maybe it's a weapon. Maybe saying what I think is the best way to finally get what I want.

"It's not actually that big of a deal, babe. It's just Walmart, and they—"

I swallow hard and cut her off. "Are an incredibly large and litigious organization that would stop at *nothing* to ruin the life of a foolish young employee," I say.

"My—" Becky says, before I cut her off too.

"I really don't mean to give you a hard time, Becky, but you need to know that Tai's real name is Yivi, and Yivi manipulated you. She steals shit all the time. She doesn't care what happens to you or her or anyone else. I love her, and I know she seems like fun, but she's a maniac." I reach over and pat Yivi's wrist. "We both are."

"Don't listen to them," Yivi says, clearly shaken by my tactics. "They're just mess—"

"No I am *not*," I say. "In fact, I *can't* mess around. I can't lie, I can't deceive, and I can't play it cool. I have taken a solemn vow of honesty, and I must speak from the heart."

"Cut it out, babe." Yivi brutalizes me with a glance, and I point my slimy smile in her direction. A combination of fear and fury flashes from the tops of her bleached brows to the bottom of her pointy chin. Too bad, so sad. I hate to do her like this, but she brought it upon herself.

"I'm sorry, Yivi, but I have to do this. These kids deserve the truth. I mean, look at us. We're adults, and we're drinking with minors. I'm hammered, you're high on pills, and we're both on the run from some creepy drug dealer dude whose fucking name is Big Gravy. I was supposed to be rich and successful and better than my father, but now my best friend is dead, and my career is in free fall, and I don't have a name, and I am hammered drunk in goddamn Missouri. I don't want to be here, I don't want to party with these children, and I don't even *like* them." I turn back to Dante and Becky. "You're weird. This motel is weird. It smells like used butt plugs, and the fish theme is tacky bullshit." I stop, winded. I collapse back into my chair. Another swallow of Captain scorches my scratchy throat, but I'm grateful for its comforting warmth. I was too dry for too long today, and it's just like Jenny used to say: *Sober doesn't match my shoes.*

"Wow, man," Becky says after a long pause. "That was literally so mean."

"But extremely impressive," Dante says, wiping chicken skin flakes from the bristles of his ratty mustache.

"If you didn't wanna hang out," Becky continues, "you coulda just said so."

"That is certainly true," Dante says. "But I sincerely love this idea of—what did you call it? A vow of honesty?"

Becky stands. "Let's get outta here, Dante," she says.

"Hold on a moment, my darling. A spoonful of radical candor never hurt anyone. If anything, I found that entire display exceedingly brave."

"*Brave*?" I ask, fighting the urge to glance at Yivi.

"Our dad would be impressed, wouldn't he, Becky?"

Becky hands Dante her empty glass. "If you're really gonna make me stay . . ." She drops back onto the couch. "Least you can do is get me another drink."

"Wait . . ." Yivi says, her tone wary and wounded. "Did you just say *our* dad?"

"She certainly did." Dante chuckles like he just let an extremely normal cat out of an extremely normal bag. "My beloved and I share a dad, but it is not quite so weird as it sounds," he continues as he swaggers toward the minibar.

"It does sound pretty fucking weird," I say, still processing the failure of my outburst.

"Our family situation might seem strange to some, but our dad is essentially a saint," Dante says over the ill-fitting shoulder of his collared shirt. "He adopted twelve children in total, all our brothers and sisters, and Becky and I are the youngest."

"Oh," I say. "Wow."

"Does he know y'all are getting married?" Yivi asks.

"Absolutely," Dante says.

"We don't keep secrets in our house," Becky adds, though it's clear she finds their home life a bit more tedious than Dante does. "It's sorta like your super-rude vow thing, except it's basically a whole lifestyle."

"Our dad likes to say *truth is a daily struggle,*" Dante says.

"Pain is the straightest path to truth," I say, quoting my own father because this is shaping up to be a highly deranged conversation, and I've got plenty of derangement to share.

"I adore that," Dante says. "And before we leave, I would love to know a bit more about you two and your journey."

Unsure how to respond, I quit into silence. My ears screech like the voices of clients who expected better. I run my palm over the plush arm of my seashell chair. Yivi won't look at me, and neither will Becky. A hot torrent of puke-flavored guilt rushes up from my guts. It batters my tonsils, and I swallow it down. I am officially willing to admit that I may have gone a little too hard with the rum this afternoon. I still want to leave, but now I can't move.

"We call it the *Circle of Trust,*" Dante says, and I stare into the peculiar boy's flapping mouth while I struggle to maintain consciousness. My sharpness has rounded, and the edges have gone off the corners of the room. Yivi, my estranged companion, has drifted further away. Her bare legs lie folded beneath her in the seashell chair. She toys with the zipper of the fannypack beached in her lap. I hope she doesn't hate me.

"We do this every Sunday in our house." Dante has returned to the fuck sofa, and he is holding Becky's hand. "But we never get the opportunity to do it with outsiders—right, Becky?"

"Sure," Becky says.

Dante grins, and his mustache quivers with self-importance. "The rules are exceedingly simple," he says. "We go around the circle three times, and each time, each of us is compelled by God and the forces of truth to reveal our inner selves with greater and greater courage. If you want, I can begin."

"Cool," Becky says, another pointedly monosyllabic response. Her humongous eyes have shrunken into her face, and suddenly she looks exactly like I feel: a hostage held captive by her own shitty choices.

"Alright, then. My first truth is that I do not always like when Becky drinks. Alcohol has a tendency to make her depressed and sometimes angry. When she entered the lobby with the two of you, I was nervous and somewhat disappointed because she has not been drunk in over three months. However, I have tolerated her decisions today because she is my sister, and I love her more than anything." Dante pauses. He nibbles his lip. "Becky, would you like to go next?"

"Sure," she says. "Fine." She guzzles her Cheapo Cruiser and hands the empty glass to Dante. "I've actually been drinking a bunch these past few months, and I wanted to come do it at your work today because I'm sick of hiding who I am just to keep you happy."

"Wonderful," Dante says, though his tone does not match his word choice. "Tai-slash-Yivi, would you like to go next?"

"Not really."

"I'll do one," I say to get her off the spot. "Mine is I *really* care about Yivi. She's my only friend in the world right now, and I feel terrible that I betrayed her trust by telling you guys all that stuff about us." I raise my fist to block a burp before continuing. "I also just want to say that I'm really sorry to y'all. I didn't need to be so rude. I was just irritated that Yivi made us come to this motel because my father has disappeared somewhere in Arkansas, and I need to get down there to help my mom kidnap him, and we're kind of in a hurry."

Dante hums with something like pleasure. "That is great. Great work. And I appreciate what you said. However, I should clarify that this is not a call-and-response sort of exercise, so just know that we cannot currently accept your apology. Also, that was technically several truths, maybe three or four, so you'll need to skip a turn."

"Y'all have lots of rules around your house, huh?" I ask.

Dante ignores me, probably to avoid the conversation I'd prefer to have. "Yivi?" he says.

"Uh, yeah, fine." She rubs her bleached eyebrows. "I guess my truth is I'm tired, and I'm getting very sick of this game."

"Same," Becky says, raising her hand.

Dante nods like a benevolent preacher. "I see." He pitches a tent with his long pinkish fingers. "Well, you can both leave if you want, but I would really appreciate if you stayed until the end of the ritual."

I open my mouth to ask what happens next in his so-called ritual, but Becky beats me to the punch. "My second truth," she says, each word bursting forth from her trembling chest, "is that I've been having sex with Jeremy!"

At this, Dante's mask of solemn composure seems to slip. His jaw falls, hang-gliding as his head spins toward Becky. His tongue twitches but fails to produce sound.

"Who's Jeremy?" Yivi asks.

"My stupid asshole manager at Walmart," Becky says, clearly on a roll. "I don't love him, and I don't wanna be fucking him, but I feel so *trapped*, you know?" Tears glisten in the corners of her ginormous eyes. "I think I wanna be with Dante, but he keeps getting more and more into the crazy shit our dad says, and I'm worried he's gonna, like, turn into him one day—or *worse*!"

"Sure," Yivi says, finally glancing at me. "We get that."

"I thought you guys did this truth thing every Sunday," I say.

"We do it in front of our whole family," Becky says. "So it's not like we can actually be honest."

"But *I* am honest!" Dante shouts.

"Bullshit!" Becky leaps to her feet. "Bullshit! Bullshit!"

"Chill, y'all," Yivi says.

"I *wanna* chill, man." Becky yanks at her pigtails. "But I feel like I'm in hell." She stomps across the room. "Our dad drives me *nuts*, and I'm terrified to tell everyone how I feel." She stands in the corner like a kid in time-out. "I hate myself, and I hate my life, and the only thing that makes anything better is drinking."

"I've got an idea," Yivi says, and I notice she is standing as well. "Let's all just chill and do a dance party."

"How do you know about the dance party?" Dante asks.

"Gimme your phone, babe," Yivi says, and while I don't understand her rationale, I point to the bed where she seems to have forgotten she left my iPhone.

"How do you know about the dance party?" Dante asks again.

Yivi flips through my phone, locating a song. "What are you talking about?" she asks.

"We always end our truth circles with a dance party," Dante says, "to help us purge any negative energy."

"Yivi is psychic," I say, suppressing a smirk as the first few bars of "Don't Stop Believin'" begin to play. "She sees the future in her dreams."

And now we're dancing, I guess. Shaking our ragged bodies in the middle of this seafoam nightmare. I slide from illustrated swordfish to clownfish as I spoil the carpet. My mind has drained back into my body, and I've regained the majority of my motor skills. Yivi, for her part, seems okay. Better than the kids. Dante and Becky are shuffling around in the corner. Not quite dancing, not quite standing. I keep peeking over there, checking to see if Becky's stopped crying. Her cheeks are wet, and her nose is running. If my heart weren't defective, it would probably go out to her. Clearly, her shit's roughly as crazy as mine, and if I'm being honest, I love that. It makes me feel less alone. In a corporate environment, where everyone used to be the captain of their high school basketball team, it was easy to forget that this whole country is full of traumatized people like me. America's recent descent into fascism has made our defects more apparent, but I can remember a time when my father's *Loose-Change*-Illuminati-flat-Earther nonsense was not fueling a full-blown culture war. Halcyon days that seem even further gone when the song changes to "Don't Stop 'Til You Get Enough," and I realize Dante is holding my phone. Perhaps they don't get the news down here in Missouri. Or perhaps Dante isn't bothered by smooth sex criminals. Either way, I've missed this song. The sad pink sun is setting over the retention pond across the highway, and dancing is better than talking. Better than thinking. Way better than rotting in my mom's Arkansas living room while she interrogates my lifestyle choices as if they are, in fact, choices.

"Babe," Yivi says, shoving her face close to mine. "You still with me?"

I swallow another sip of rum and give Yivi my full attention. "I'm here, aren't I?" I say.

"You seem super out of it."

I squint at her mouth. Far as I can tell, I'm dancing in my usual way: Like I'm running to catch a very slow bus. Lifting my knees, pumping my arms, rotating in a loose circle. Not exactly J-Hope, but reasonably socially acceptable. "I'm just trying to enjoy myself."

"I get it, babe," Yivi says, lowering her voice so only I can hear. "They're weird. This is weird. It's my fault we stopped. I'm sorry about it, and I promise we can leave as soon as I'm sure Becky's okay."

"*Chill*, Yivi," I say. "Slow it down. I'm fine to keep dancing until I'm done sobering up."

"Is that what you call this?" She nods at the bottle still clutched in my paw.

"If I rush straight to the surface, I'll get the bends."

Yivi's eyes disappear into her face, but I'm positive she's rolling them behind her eyelids. Regardless, we continue to groove. Dante claps when the song changes. I don't recognize this one right away, but when I hear the words *we* and *are* and *family*, I figure it out pretty quick.

"This shit is so Toddamn weird, I can't even take it," Yivi says, shaking her head.

"I do bet Todd loves adoptive-family incest." I almost laugh, but I don't. I have more important things to deal with. "Hey, Yivi?" I say.

"Yeah? What?"

"I just wanted to say sorry again for telling them about Big Gravy and all that."

"You're just lucky they're ding-dongs."

"Are you mad about it?"

"Not really." She pauses. "What about you?"

"I have completely forgiven you, if that's what you're asking."

"Then why do you still seem so grumpy?"

"Hard to say."

Yivi bobs to the beat, and the bouncy bounce of her curly hair contradicts the furrow in her forehead. "Maybe you'd feel better if you paused your drinking and tried something else." She pats her fannypack.

"I've already got enough shit messing with my head."

"But that's the point," Yivi says. "Q chases all your icky little moodies away."

"Are you sure *your* icky moodies are on the run, at present?"

"Don't be a dick."

"But I'm so unbelievably good at it," I say, forcing some sarcastic pep into my step. I Travolta away and float on the music. I bop, hop, and roll. Since I last checked their status, the kids have begun to hug, swaying to the music as if it's a slow song at prom, and I don't know why, but I'm a tad jealous. Not of their hugging, obviously, but their affection. Their real shot at love. It makes me miss Jenny more than Clinton, but way beyond that, it makes me wish I still believed in certain nonsense.

"Cut it out," Yivi says, pouncing toward me. She knots six or seven of her spidery limbs around my gyrating waist, holding me close against my will. "I'm serious, babe," she continues. "I hate fighting."

"Then let's call a truce," I say, losing my balance. I stumble, and Yivi holds fast to keep me from falling. I can tell she thinks

I'm a teeny-tad overserved, but that's fine. People have thought that before.

"You're a disaster," she says, confirming my suspicions.

I grin with all my big, gorgeous teeth. "But at least it's a controlled demolition," I say.

"I really can't tell what you're thinking sometimes."

"Likewise." I shrug. "But I still love you."

"I love you too," Yivi says with a startling lack of hesitation.

"That's not what I meant."

Yivi tilts her head but doesn't respond. I stare deep into her fiercely curious eyes. The song has changed again, but the lyrics are alien languages. Outside, darkness has dropped over the parking lot. A black ribbon of highway flaps into the sky. It calls to me like a mother. I sigh and shift closer to Yivi, and her expression softens. Our dancing slows but the music doesn't. I have this strange feeling like tonight might be the last nice night of my life.

"What are you so smiley about all of a sudden?" Yivi asks.

"Nothing." I cover her spiky shoulders with my palms. "You're great."

"I am?"

I nod, though I only said *great* because it was the first word that came to mind. "Yeah. You're cool. Thanks for putting up with me."

Yivi gives me a withering-yet-playful glare that I think is intended to be flirtatious. "Why're you getting so mushy?"

"I don't know," I say, searching for the reason. "I guess I'm ready to say goodbye."

"To these guys?"

I shake my head as I realize what's happening. I peck Yivi a kiss on the cheek, and then, with my mouth near her ear, I tell her, "I really don't think you should come to Arkansas."

She flinches like I slapped her. "What?" She stops dancing, and I freeze.

"I think this is it for us," I say. "For your own good."

"Are you fucking with me?"

I shake my head. *Brave* is not an adjective I would self-apply, but I feel it now. A deep acceptance, maybe. Who I am, where I'm headed, why I need to go alone. "You want to know why I'm running from the cops, right?" I ask, chanting so my words join the music. "Well, I'll tell you. I killed my best friend two weeks ago, Yivi. Her name was Jenny, and I killed her. I know you've seen some shit, but you don't need these problems, okay?"

My admission crashes headlong into Yivi's face, and her guardrails crumple. "You seriously killed your friend?" she asks.

"I did, yeah. And I'm sorry I didn't tell you before we left Chicago. I was scared."

"But why?" She takes a tiny step backward. "Why the fuck would you do that?"

"I didn't exactly mean to."

"It was an accident?"

"Don't worry about it, okay? I've already said too much, and what you don't know can't hurt you."

"What's happening?" Becky asks, and I turn. She and Dante are awash in a whirling bath of blue and red light. Their cherubic faces flash with concern, then confusion, then amusement. I steel myself with another swig of rum, but by the time I'm ready to tell them I'm leaving, I realize the kids aren't looking at me, and they aren't looking at Yivi.

"Whoa, guys—*look*!" Becky says, shouting over the music. She and Dante stride past us to the window. There they pose like *Titanic*, like Kate and Leo on the bow, and stare down at the parking lot. Without waiting for me, Yivi hustles to their vantage point.

"Oh, fuck fucking fuck," she says.

I stumble past her as the red and blue lights, which I'd assumed were an exciting new symptom of my brain damage, take on a much more tangible significance. "You *did* dream a parking lot," I say to Yivi, when I spot the police. Two squad cars and three cops milling around the M2, one on her radio, and the other two headed for the motel's front entrance. Looks like Clinton finally reported his car stolen.

"This happens," Dante says, beaming with what seems like personal pride. "We get an inordinate number of fugitives at this Motel 6. Sometimes I help the authorities raid their rooms."

"They're looking for—" I start, but Yivi snatches my wrist. Suddenly, I am here, and I am now. "Who do you think they're looking for?" I ask.

"That is difficult to say," Dante says, enjoying the mystery. "Though it usually has something to do with drugs . . ."

Becky's eyes regain their sober enormity as she scrutinizes my face. "Wait," she says, "isn't that you guys' car?"

"The stupid blue one?" I tap my chin with a thoughtful finger. "Yeah, I think it is. Why do you ask?"

"Didn't you, like, mention something about a drug dealer?" Becky edges closer to her fiancé. I am happy to see their relationship is healing, but when her hip knocks into his, Dante's self-righteous cheer melts away. An unpleasant series of calculations and realizations flashes across his face, and I brace myself. Clearly, Dante is a Good Samaritan. The type of romantic idiot who gets shot chasing shoplifters from convenience stores. His back straightens, and he puffs his chest. He may be small, but I'm on a losing streak. In a fight for my life, I'd probably let him win.

"I'm really sorry about this," Yivi says, and I notice with some concern that she is now wielding her large black hunting knife. "You guys have been super chill, and I just need to make sure you don't try anything stupid, okay?"

"The fucking what are you doing, Yivi?" I ask, speaking faster than my tongue can arrange my words.

"We're not bad people," Yivi continues. "We're just in a bad situation, and we need you guys to be cool."

Becky is shaking. "Dante . . . do something . . ."

"Tell your bitch to be cool, Dante," Yivi says.

"Becky is not a bitch," Dante says without fear. "She is my sister and my one true love."

"Everybody calm down," I say. "Put the knives away—and stop calling people bitches."

"Do you guys have a car?" Yivi asks.

"Why have these cops come looking for you?" Dante asks.

"We stole my ex-boyfriend's BMW," I say.

Becky, probably because all that eyeball makes her extra perceptive, doesn't seem to believe the car is the whole of it. "What about the drug dealer?" she asks.

Yivi lurches forward with her knife. "No more fucking questions," she says, stabbing the air near Becky's face. "Give us a car, or I swear to Christ, I'll kill you. I'll do it, and I won't even be sorry."

"She isn't going to kill you," I say.

"We—we have a car," Becky says. "It's Dante's, but we share it."

"Love to hear it." Yivi extends her free hand toward Dante. "Now give me the keys, and nobody gets hurt."

Dante leads the way down six flights of maintenance stairs. Yivi keeps her knife trained on the base of Becky's neck, and I lag behind, struggling to keep pace with their descent. This unexpected cardio isn't agreeing with my booze-numb knees. A nervous fire in my belly burns like the time my father woke my brother and I in the middle of the night, saying we had to go, Mom was in the car, and the bioweapons had already eradicated most of Chicago. This was before smartphones, so we made it halfway across Iowa before Mom mentioned the atrocity to an attendant at a rest stop, and he looked at my whole family like we were the nuttiest nuts in the world.

"I would really appreciate if you might consider putting that knife away," Dante says when we near the first floor. "I promise to give you the car without a struggle."

"No can do, Ringo," Yivi says.

We reach the bottom of the musty stairwell, and I lean against a cold steel handrail, panting. The stairway is badly lit, which seems on-brand for a Motel 6, and the bloodred glow of an EXIT sign lends Yivi's curls a spooky sparkle. She backs Dante and Becky against a cinder-block wall. "I don't normally like leaving witnesses," she says, and Becky gasps.

"Cut the crap, Yivi," I say. "They already said we could have the car."

"But how do we know they're not gonna rat?"

"I swear we won't," Becky says with a shaky voice.

I give the girl what I hope is a reassuring look. My recent sins are beginning to read like a Buzzfeed listicle, and it was not my intention to add traumatizing children and armed robbery to my hypothetical rap sheet. I don't know what Yivi is doing. I don't know why she is doing it. I don't know anything about her, and I have no idea what she's capable of. When I confessed to Jenny's murder, I assumed that would be the end of this Yivi-filled chapter of my ludicrous little life. Maybe I even hoped that was the case. But now I'm not so sure.

"I hope you don't mind me saying so," Dante says, with just the slightest hint of fear in his voice. "But you both seem to have forgotten your clothes."

Yivi looks down. "Oh fuck."

Oh fuck is right. In our haste, we neglected to change out of these ridiculous bathrobes. I managed to remember a bottle of Captain, my wallet, my iPhone, and my Balenciaga shoes, but the rest of my wardrobe is balled up on the bathroom floor. "Oops," I say, because I'm wasted and also a moron.

Yivi glares as if this whole situation is entirely my fault. "How the fuck are we gonna get to Arkansas in fucking bathrobes?" she says, and as she says it, Dante moves.

The knife hits the floor. It bounces here, there, elsewhere, and I scream. Becky screams too. Dante wrestles Yivi onto the stairs. She shouts for me to grab the knife. Dante shouts something similar to Becky, but I kick his fiancée in the face as she scrabbles across the floor. Soccer reflexes. With a yelp, Becky flops sideways, and I hope I haven't killed her.

"I am now holding the knife," I announce, and everyone stops struggling. They all look somewhere between angry and afraid, even Yivi, but I am too busy being thankful that Becky is alive to worry about Yivi's lack of team spirit.

"I am holding the knife," I repeat. "But I don't plan to use it." I allow the blade to hang limp by my side. "I'm very sorry that my incredibly chaotic friend has threatened you guys, and in exchange for your car and your forgiveness, I want to give you some money."

"Money?" Dante is leaning against the wall.

"How much money?" Yivi is sitting on the stairs.

"You kicked me in the head." Becky is kneeling near my feet.

I slip the knife into the pocket of my robe, and my fingers close around my wallet. I remove my debit card and hold it next to my ear. Clinton was always scolding me to open a savings account so all my money wouldn't be in one place, and now I'm glad I didn't listen. It makes what I'm about to do a lot more dramatic.

"I have roughly a hundred thousand dollars in this bank account," I say. "If you take this card to an ATM, you can have all the money you want. All I ask is that you give us your car, promise not to tell anyone what happened here, and use my money to get as far away from your dad as possible before he ruins the rest of your stupid lives."

"We would never turn our backs on our dad," Dante says.

"Shut up, Dante," Becky says.

"That's *everything*, babe," Yivi says.

"I'm really sorry I kicked you in the head," I say as I offer the card for Becky to take.

She peers up at me, and I can see her wrestling with the girl she is and the girl she wants to be. I know the general feeling.

"Why do you want us to get away from our dad?" she asks, but I don't respond right away. Instead, I think about Mom screaming that we were going to lose our house. I think about my father bingeing *Coast to Coast AM* while we ate rice and beans every night for months. I think about Clinton spending my money because he hated asking his rich daddy for funds. I think about working eighty-hour weeks for ten years, saving half of every paycheck, lying and cheating and placating phonies. I think about the calm, normal, middle-class American life

I've been dreaming of since I was a kid. I want that life for poor young Becky. She deserves it more than me.

"You know why," I say.

"But we don't want your money," Dante says.

"I don't want your car either, Dante, but I'm taking it."

I glance at Yivi. Unsurprisingly, she's staring daggers bigger than her hunting knife. She'd probably prefer I stole this car on principle, but I've made my decision.

"Thank you," Becky says after a seemingly endless moment, and I can tell we understand each other. She takes my card, and I give her my PIN.

"It's the little red hatchback," Dante says.

I shove open the emergency door. Yivi's Doc Martens smack pavement behind me. The vast empty parking lot fills me with dread. Every shadow could be a cop. I scan the cars, pickups, minivans, my hope burning down to nearly nothing before I spot a cherry-red Toyota Corolla crouching in the shadow of a storage shed, and I suddenly feel free. For several semi-wonderful seconds, I imagine that me, Yivi, Dante, Becky, and all the rest of humanity's children might one day come together to right the great and horrible wrongs perpetrated by our fathers, and the thought makes me want to cry. Then, I get a closer look at the car I just spent my entire life savings on, and the lump in my throat explodes like a laugh.

FOUR

I awaken with a gasp, white-knuckling a steering wheel. A few blurry seconds race past, and I wonder if Dante and Becky were a dream. But this steering wheel doesn't have a fuzzy red cover, and the ghost of a billboard up ahead screams JOIN THE ARKANSAS NATIONAL GUARD. I must have fallen asleep driving. Good thing Yivi is shrieking in the backseat again. If it weren't for her psychic night terrors, I probably would have wrapped this car around a tree.

I wipe a hot dribble of drool from the corner of my mouth and rub my raw eyes till they're significantly rawer. The clock on the dash could be significantly brighter, but I think it says 2:53. The pain in my head is unbelievable, worse than ever, and my body is alive with sensations: skin-crawling weirdness, foreign body parts, achy joints. I wish I could strip naked, peel off this scratchy bathrobe and toss it out the window, but I'd probably get pulled over for littering. A little less than twenty-four hours on the road, and I'm already broke and vaguely broken. I should wake Yivi and make her drive, but she hasn't spoken to me since we left the motel.

I reach into the torn-up passenger seat, fondling the crusty gray fabric until my hand finds what's left of our Captain Morgan. A few precious drops. I sip and sigh. It's dark as hell out here. Total blackness aside from the yellow lines dividing the road. I suck a long ragged breath. The Google Maps countdown says three more hours.

None of what I fear.

None of what I fear.

None of what I fear.

My fingers twitch as Yivi screams again. And again. Clipped yipping sounds that bother my blood and conjure another of my father's oddball mottos: *Die screaming*. Scratch and slash to your last breath. Some *Braveheart* "FREEDOM" bullshit. Needlessly dramatic, but one of his better policies in my opinion. I've often wished I could live that way, but it's hard to be uncompromising. Hard to say no when the world says yes. Easier to kiss some asses and stay with Clinton and listen to Jenny. I've always thought my father would be a more impressive person if he practiced his own preachings, but lately I'm not so sure. I haven't exactly died screaming, but I've made more than a couple mistakes these past few days. Rode my own drama too far, too hard. For one thing, I probably should've left Yivi back at the motel. For another, this piece-of-shit Corolla is barely fit to drive.

A louder Yivi scream fills the car, and I flip the headlights to brights, squinting through the bug-smeared windshield. Cars are a mechanical mystery to me, but this one definitely sucks. It's greasy with slime in the cupholders. The dashboard rattles if I go above forty. The tires jump if I hit the smallest bump. The seats smell like chocolate dog tumors. And there's a hole underneath the gas pedal, offering a view of the cracked asphalt racing beneath my feet.

A new thought on a loop:

I need to get back to work.

I need to get back to work.

I need to get back to work.

I smack my skull against the headrest to knock the mantra loose, but the impact only strengthens my headache.

"NEEOH," Yivi screams, punching my seat. "NEOH. NOH. NO."

"WAKE THE FUCK UP, YIVI!" I yell, and my face explodes with a hot flash of pain. I almost vomit. The road fuzzes out of view, and for a moment, I'm blind again. My breath catches in my throat, and my heart hammers my sour guts. Foreshocks of a panic attack.

"DON'T DO IT!" Yivi screams, and I tap the brakes. Time to stop. A gas station glows on the edge of the highway, and I angle the car toward an exit.

"WE'LL NEVER MAKE IT!" Yivi screams, even louder this time. I glance over my shoulder, but she isn't talking to me. I jam my thumb into the dent above my ear and focus on my breath.

"It's just a dream, Yiv," I say as she continues to batter my seat. "And I really hope this one doesn't come true."

I whip the Corolla into the corner of a gravel lot, parking as far away from the Happy Stop Gas Shop as possible. Yivi has begun kicking the back door with both feet. I've penned enough commercials for Toyota to know that their cars have a great IIHS Crash Safety Rating, but I doubt this particular Corolla can handle Yivi's interior assault. I've been told that you aren't supposed to rouse someone from a night terror, but I've grown accustomed to waking Yivi because the elderly woman who owned our Airbnb threatened to evict her if Yivi didn't stop scaring her dogs.

"Yiv, goddamnit—chill out." I grab her shoulder, shaking until her fingers close around my arm and her chipped black nails dig into my flesh. "HEY," I yell, and her eyes pop open.

She rubs her eyelids. "The fuck did you wake me?"

"You sounded like you were dying." I inspect my arm, glad Yivi didn't break skin. My mom clawed my father's neck once during one of their monthly brawls, and he still has the scars.

"I wasn't dying," Yivi says, rolling over and shoving her sour face into the seat cushion. "I was winning."

"More cops?"

"This time it was forest priests."

"Forest *what*?"

"None of your business."

"What about your cowboy friend?"

"Do we have anything worth drinking?"

"Negative," I say. "That's why I've ferried us here to this wonderful establishment."

The Happy Stop Gas Shop is a lopsided gray structure with bars on the windows. The lot is empty except for our car, and we're light-years away from anything resembling civilization. Aside from a dim glow filtering through the Jack Daniels ads pasted over the windows, the only proof of life is the red-white-and-blue shine of the HAPPY STOP sign looming over the highway.

"I feel like itchy buttholes," Yivi says.

"Are you gonna pout the rest of this trip?"

"Fuck off." She rolls onto her back and unzips her fannypack. After some fiddling, she dry swallows two pills. I'm tempted to ask for a dose this time, but I'll need all my mental faculties intact when I go toe-to-toe with Mom in a couple hours.

I restart the car, throw it in reverse, and drive over to the sole gas pump that isn't out of order. There's no computer screen or card reader. A pay-inside situation, I guess. "I'm going in for some booze," I say.

"You and what money?"

I leaf through my wallet and move my Chili's gift card where my debit used to be. The Chili's card was a gift from Jenny. We had a long-running birthday joke where we never gave each other anything other than a fifty-dollar gift card to our favorite restaurant. The food at Chili's is obviously trash, but we knew we'd never run into coworkers. It was there that we plotted our promotions, bemoaned our shitty childhoods, scheduled two emergency abortions, debated the pros and cons of rehab, and admitted our complicated feelings for each other. We were actually eating baby back ribs the day I told Jenny about my potential genderqueerness. Yivi was the second person I ever told, but Jenny was the first, so I guess you could say I came out at Chili's. "I've still got a hundred or so left," I say when I've finished checking every corner of my wallet for emergency twenties.

"Okay," Yivi says. "Gimme."

"Why?"

Yivi extends her palm, bored and cold. "Gimme the money, and I'll do the shopping."

"But *why*?"

"You're wearing a bathrobe, and you look unhoused."

"So do you."

Yivi gives me a small black smirk. "But at least I make it look like a choice."

I shove open my door and sit with my legs hanging out of the car. I roll the parking lot gravel around under my shit-beat Balenciaga sneakers. The stains have faded, but drops of blood still dot my formerly white shoelaces. *Thanks, Clinton.*

I press my palms into my eyes. Anxiety rises as my drunkenness ebbs. I tell myself I'll be okay because I'm not my father. I just need a few good nights of sleep. Healthy food to settle my stomach. More time to make a decent plan. I'll ditch dirtbag Yivi, locate AWOL Henry, and find a way to clear my deadname. Money is officially tight, but I feel better without it, free at last from the evils of ambition, and I have always been great at talking. With a good-boy crew cut and a suit as blue as my eyes, I could try to represent myself in court. I could explain how I didn't mean to kill Jenny. I'm pretty short on character witnesses, but my story is sympathetic. Rags to riches to reckless homicide. An underdog fighting for their life. My queerness might hurt my case, but if I'm going to reenter society, I need to be real. I need to bounce my tight hot ass on the rock-hard mercy of the universe.

I also need to get it all sorted in my head. How Jenny and I were up for a huge promotion, but she was hurtling toward a breakdown. We were on a work trip to Cleveland for an important new business pitch, and Jenny forgot to pack her Xanax. She was coming down from a pretty protracted cocaine binge. She kept dissolving into tears, saying she couldn't do the client meeting. We were so close to our goal, but Jenny was trying to faceplant at the finish line. So, yeah, I texted some people, and I found a benzo connect in Cleveland. It didn't seem sketchy until I took an Uber across the city to a creepy flophouse where a large, toothless white dude sold me some shit he said was *probably* Valium. Then I lied, and I told Jenny the drugs were safe.

My motives were incredibly selfish and, let me be clear, essentially unforgivable, but what I did wasn't inherently evil.

I may be an asshole, a fuckup, and an addict, but actions aside, I am not a murderer. I still know, or at least believe, that there is good in me. I think I can be saved from the vestigial parts of my identity, the greedy, hateful American parts I started to shed when I finally stopped being a liar, a man, and my father's son. I understand how it looks, and I understand what I did, but if I could explain myself, if I could tell the right truth the right way, the way it all actually happened, then I think a jury of my so-called peers might forgive me. This may be a mostly bad country run by mostly bad people, but I think it might be possible for some of us, maybe even me, to become good. We can make things right and atone for our past. I have long wondered why the fuck I am alive, but I'm beginning to think I was put here to tell a bigger truth. Our truth. To carve away the rotten bits of my festering mind with the Occam's razor of the better angels of my greater nature. And while I am 100 percent positive that last thought did not make any fucking sense, it certainly felt true when I thought it, and that matters. That truth matters. It is my real destination by way of Arkansas. Todd take the wheel of Dante's rat-mobile. I will find it, or I will die screaming. My brain is fucked, my wallet is empty, but my heart is as full as my bladder.

A gasoline breeze knocks up, the fumes kissing my tongue. A plastic THANK YOU FOR SHOPPING bag clings to the barbwire fence rimming the property. The bag rustles as the wind moves through, and my urge to urinate becomes impossible to ignore.

I stand and search for something inoffensive to piss on. Something that won't get me shot by onlooking hillbilly snipers. Foliage. I stumble toward a short leafless bush separating the parking lot from a spooky snarl of forest, my groin pulsating with every step. I peek back at the Happy Stop Gas Shop's front door, but there's no sign of Yivi. Thank Todd. I need a Yivi break almost as bad as I need a piss. If I weren't trying so hard to be a better person, I would abandon her garbage-goth ass as soon as I've relieved myself. That said, I'm glad she offered to shop because I hate the creeps who work at gas stations. My father used to drive downtown Chicago for work, and his shitty blue Cutlass would crap out constantly. One night, Mom took us out to search for him because he was stranded, but we didn't have cellphones, and she couldn't remember which gas station he'd called from. We drove to three different places on North Avenue before she started freaking out in the parking lot of an Amoco, saying we'd never find him. I was only eight or nine at the time, but Mom sent me into the convenience store to ask if I could borrow a phone to call all the other gas stations in the area, and the potbellied dude behind the counter told me I could only use his phone if I gave him a hug.

I reach the bush, snatch up my dick, and unleash a tremendous stream. It's wondrous, like cheating on your boyfriend with your creative partner, but my pleasure is interrupted by a tingling sensation, my scaredy-sense telling me I'm being observed.

I whip out my iPhone and flick on my flashlight. I pan the woods, checking for boogeymen and Peeping Tom Sawyers and whoever Yivi mentioned earlier—*forest priests*—but the only eyes I see belong to a giant bird. It calls to me, once, and flaps off into the darkness. I watch it leave and swat a mosquito that lands on my bicep. I hate skeeters because they're just like my father. They make zero attempts to coexist peacefully with humanity. I miss smashing the bloodsucker, but I successfully dribble piss onto my robe. I sigh and retie my belt as a wide swath of light explodes behind my back.

Wheeling around, I cover my eyes against the glare of headlights. I shine my meager flashlight at the car to discern the color. All signs point to tan.

I stand frozen like an itty-bitty deer baby—or the moose my father annihilated on our road trip to Idaho—but I don't know why. I've still got Yivi's big grisly knife in my pocket, and I'm sick of playing scared.

One of the more dysfunctional things my father likes to say when the going gets tough is: *I may be walking through the valley of the shadow of death, but I fear no evil because I am the meanest son of a bitch in the valley.* And he's not wrong. My father is my size, five-ten, 190, but when he goes berserk, no member of polite society will test him. He can back down drunks, intimidate soldiers, and scare the shit out of anyone who decides to test his road rage in traffic. He is the kind of man who gets out of his car to wrestle truck drivers even when his children are in the backseat, and when kids used to argue whose dad would win in a fight, I would stay quiet because the point was moot. Ferocity is my father's superpower, a psychosis he can switch on but not necessarily off, and maybe I possess similar abilities. Maybe I should brandish this hunting knife and chase Big Gravy's cowboy comrade out of town. Or maybe Yivi just exited the Happy Stop Gas Shop at top speed, and I should follow her lead by running like hell for our car.

I dash through the night, pumping my arms and legs like Tom Cruise if he were a queer and drunken disaster. It's a short distance, but I haven't sprinted flat out since the aughts. By the time Yivi notices me, my lungs are burning, my spine is rattling, and my knees are shot.

"RUN, YIVI! IT'S THE COWBOY GUY!"

"WHAT?" she hollers, hot on my heels.

"STOP! THIEF!" shouts an unfamiliar voice.

I whip my head around to watch an angry round woman emerge from the Happy Stop Gas Shop toting a hunting rifle. A gunshot rings out, and I lose my footing in the gravel, slipping and sliding into a graceless somersault that skins my knees and slices my ass.

"DID YOU STEAL SOMETHING?!" I shout as I scramble to my feet.

"DID YOU SAY *COWBOY GUY*?!" Yivi shouts back.

"YOU KNOW I FUCKING DID!" I dive into the driver's seat and start the car. A millisecond later, Yivi leaps into the backseat. Another gunshot cracks the air. Yivi's door slams, and I smash the gas pedal.

Our tires spin, tossing gravel until we find purchase. The Corolla lurches forward. I weave left, right, and center. My driver's side mirror explodes, and I duck under the sound of another pair of gunshots. Yivi screams, and we fishtail hard as I swerve out of the parking lot, escaping with what's left of our lives.

I skid hard through a turn and accelerate onto a road leading into some foothills. I race past rows of lifeless trailers and wheelless trucks rusting in tall grass. At the next intersection, I make another random turn, slower this time because the Corolla is making death rattles. We need to be smart, and smart isn't exactly my topmost skill these days.

"Babe?" Yivi asks, poking her head between the front seats.

"Put your safety belt on."

"Are you gonna tell me what happened back there?"

"How the fuck should I know?" I hang a sloppy right down another unmarked street, and Yivi flops onto the floor with a yelp. The bottles she so cleverly acquired at the Happy Stop Gas Shop clank and clatter. Which reminds me: I'd suck James David Vance for a drink.

Yivi crawls back into her seat. "Where the hell are you going?"

"I asked you to put your safety belt on," I say, because my goal is to make us impossible to follow, but I'm not an expert in counter-surveillance, and I don't feel like explaining myself.

Yivi grunts but her safety belt clicks. "This is fucking ridiculous, babe."

I punch the brake and drift onto an even darker and emptier street. No houses, no cars, no people. A road to nowhere built for seemingly no reason. I check my two remaining mirrors. I don't see any headlights, and I wish that made me feel better. "I strongly disagree," I say.

"Okay." Yivi scoffs. "Cool."

"What's *actually* fucking ridiculous, Yivi, is that you got caught shoplifting for no reason," I say, before casually adding: "AND I ALMOST GOT SHOT BY A FUCKING COWBOY!"

We drive a few hours in rotten silence, Yivi sitting slumped like Wednesday Addams in the backseat, me not giving a shit because I don't give a shit. She can pout, and I can wait her out. And besides, I refuse to feel bad this time. For one, I should be allowed to yell when bullets are involved. For two, I told her she could stay in Missouri. Nobody asked her to follow me into this car. That was her shit, and as far as I'm concerned, she is responsible for her own displeasure. And mine.

I zigzag through another half-dead Arkansas town I can't

even see on the map. The sky is nauseous with the coming sun. The houses are forgotten and gray. I wonder how it might feel to wake up in this sad stretch of America every day for the rest of my life. Not awesome, probably. My mom doesn't belong in a place like this, but she also doesn't realize she deserves better. I have always sensed a nascent grandeur about her—like a great artist who has chosen advertising because they lack the confidence and family fortune to move to New York and blow their parents' money buying friends who will support their dogshit scribblings.

Jenny was also like that. She often reminded me of my mom. She was roughly five years older than me—and a lot wiser. Our partnership was always based on something more than creative compatibility. Understanding was part of it, repression was a feature, and attraction factored in, but I also looked up to her. Despite her chronic lack of self-esteem, Jenny was incredible at her job. She understood culture, what made things cool, and how to turn coolness into sales. The instant I met her, I knew she was the best creative at our agency. She had another partner at the time, this pothead hypedouche called Tommy. They were universally considered the agency's best team, but I could see Jenny was the star player. It was easy to break them up. I just made Jenny my friend and told her Tommy was talking shit behind her back. This was a necessary lie. We needed each other. I was a striver and a way better writer than Tommy, and Jenny was my meal ticket. I knew that, together, we could make it to the top. I just didn't realize how strongly Jenny believed she belonged at the bottom.

"We gonna turn this shit back into a party or not, babe?" Yivi says, shattering our silence. Behind me, she holds up a two-liter Sprite and a fifth of Smirnoff. The key ingredients for our beloved Birthday Cakes. A peace offering that I am prepared to accept due to necessity and a strong desire to stop remembering Jenny.

"Let's get turnt." I pat the passenger seat. "Want to come up here, so we can talk while you mix?"

"You're not gonna yell anymore?"

"I hate to yell, Yivi," I say, and it's very true. Clinton loved to raise his voice, but I usually refused to engage. Yelling is for losers like my parents, and I prefer to hide the fact I was raised poor and angry. "I'm just slowly coming to terms with you being a total maniac," I continue. "And my yelling is residual disillusion gradually leaving my body."

"That's a pretty complicated way to admit you've been acting like a dick since yesterday morning."

"*You* forced us to stop at a motel."

"Because *you* clearly needed a rest."

"*You* made me hang out with those insane children."

"Because *you* wouldn't tell me why you're on the run from the cops."

"*You* threatened to stab the insane but mostly friendly children with a giant knife."

"Because *you* made me an accessory to murder, and I don't wanna go back to prison."

I pause to consider the flow of her logic, and surprisingly, it checks out. In some ways, it makes her sound significantly more rational than me. "Fine," I say, deciding not to ask her why she was in prison. "But there's no excuse for stealing that stuff."

"Are you kidding?" Yivi asks as she wriggles over the center console and settles cross-legged into her copilot chair. The hem of her robe rides up, exposing a neat row of razor blade scars on the inside of her thigh. I've never seen these before. I wait for her to say something more, but she doesn't. Instead, she produces a pair of paper coffee cups from a THANK YOU FOR SHOPPING bag and busies herself mixing the optimal ratio of Sprite, Mountain Dew Code Red, and vodka.

"No, Yiv," I say. "As a rule, I am not kidding until further notice."

"Excuse me for trying to pinch some pennies after you traded all the rest of our money for a poo-poo-scented beater that can barely handle the highway."

My left eyebrow, which is traditionally bitchier than its twin, crawls halfway up my forehead. "What do you mean *our* money?" I ask.

All at once, a splotchy red rash covers Yivi's tan cheeks. I guess she is blushing, and I'm surprised. I don't think I've ever seen her embarrassed before. "I meant *your* money," she says.

"Did you?"

"I definitely did."

I roll a stop sign and hang a jerky left onto a wasted gravel road that Google Maps seems to think won't dead-end in a haunted cluster of *Winter's Bone*–style meth huts. "Then we agree it's *my* money, and I'm sure we also agree that I can do whatever the fuck I want with it."

"True." Yivi hands me a drink. "I'm sorry I said that."

I wait for her to continue, but she doesn't. Which is fine. I don't blame her for thinking I would keep her fed and watered or whatever. Pretty sure I promised as much. But it's an extremely long walk from *needing* my money to *having* my money, regardless of her intellectual disposition toward the concept of property. "Is that why you didn't talk to me all night?" I ask.

Yivi continues to ruminate while she pours. The radio in this shit box keeps fritzing in and out, but the vodka drumming the bottom of Yivi's paper cup is music enough for me. The smell as well. A Birthday Cake is a beautiful thing, a drink mixologized when Yivi and I realized Sprite plus vodka almost tasted like cake batter, and my head feels better already.

"I didn't talk to you all night," she says finally, "because you're a friend-killer who tried to abandon me in Missouri, and I'm still working through how I feel about that." She pauses and hands me a cup. "It's just weird that you've been giving me all this shit about honesty, but you were withholding that pretty essential slice of info, you know?"

"I'll tell you the rest of the story if you really want," I say as I bring the drink to my lips. Sweet relief fizzes into my nose, and for a little while, I almost forget where we're headed. I escape my body, gliding above the car as we shake, rattle, and roll. It might sound odd, given that I rarely stop drinking these days, but whenever I make the mistake of sobering up, my next first sip always takes me right back to junior high. I was twelve, I think, and it was Christmastime. My father had this carpenter buddy named Chuck, Chuck Steinbacher, and Chuck was an alcoholic. More than that, though, Chuck was a nearly normal guy. Proof positive that my father could make socially acceptable friends. Chuck had lost his thumb playing moped chicken when he was a kid, and when I knew him, he was living with a woman old enough to be his mother. I can't remember her name, but they were sort of a couple. They would have these holiday parties where Chuck would show off his model-train collection, all the tracks weaving between the presents under the Christmas tree. My brother was younger, and he loved that shit. I, on the other hand, loved that Chuck snuck me drinks. At first, it was a nip here or there, but the year I turned twelve, Chuck made me an Amaretto Stone Sour. I have since realized that my first-ever cocktail probably tasted a lot like its acronym, but that Christmas, the orange almond piss was fucking magic. My mom had abandoned my brother and me a few days before the party. She came back several weeks later, but at the time, I was staring down the barrel of a single-father future, and I drank my first glass fast, and my second one faster. I lost count pretty quick after that, drinking the Amaretto straight because I was alone in the kitchen and couldn't remember the recipe. Some time later, I regained consciousness on my back, dazed on Chuck's couch, slick with my own sick. My father was furious, and I never saw Chuck again after that. Mom eventually told me he died of liver failure when I was in high school, but in my darkest and drunkest moments, I always come back to the reassuring mental image of Chuck's dummy smile, his thumbless hand on my shoulder, and his voice saying, *I've been here, kid.*

"I do want," Yivi says as my drink disappears, and I return my cup to her lap.

"Your wish is my command," I say, so as not to jeopardize my incoming refill, and then, without further ado, I begin.

Shortly after dawn, my armpits are still damp from my confession, and we stop for gas at a shimmering BP perched high on an optimistic overpass, the crown jewel in a gaudy new-construction rest stop that promises a brighter future for Arkansas. Our tank's been on *E* the past twenty miles, so the stop wasn't optional. I'm sure I look completely fucking unhinged bumbling through the convenience store in my bathrobe, but Yivi has lost her paying privileges. I fork over six dollars a gallon, the rest of our money, but my empty wallet feels like penance.

"Think we're safe for a nap?" Yivi asks when I restart the engine. We've had a pretty chill ride since I told her the truth about Jenny, and I guess I shouldn't be surprised. I may have tastefully omitted the fact that I bought the drugs so Jenny wouldn't fuck up our client meeting, but compared to Yivi's mysterious and myriad crimes, my accidental murder probably seemed pretty piddly. Either way, I'm grateful for her understanding. I doubt anyone else in my life would have received my tale so well.

"Let's give it a shot," I say as I idle over and park us behind a Taco Bell. Yivi drops to sleep before I've even turned off the car, but I stay awake for another forty-five minutes, drinking away the rest of my headache. It helps, but the sugar bothers my stomach. A searing heat rises in my neck. I depress the window control with my middle finger, and the glass stutters downward, squeaking with exertion until the mechanism quits. In a silent fury, I wrestle the glass, jamming the panel lower until it disappears into the door.

A weak summer breeze licks my throat, but the air's too damp to offer much relief. Fuck it. I crank back my seat.

I open my eyes. The sun rushes against my face and stops there, buzzing like the wings of a wasp. I reach for my leftover Birthday Cake, and it hurts to move my arm, hurts to lift the drink, hurts to swallow the cool.

I blink at the dashboard clock. It's a quarter after two. My iPhone vibrates—a new text from Mom. Something is stabbing my hip. I stash Yivi's big knife in the door pocket and look over at my friend. Still dozing. Abnormally peaceful. Her silly cat-head necklace rises and falls with every breath. Part of me thinks I need her. Another part of me suspects she was sent here to punish me for my sins.

"Fuck you looking at?" Yivi asks, reanimating.

"Nothing," I say with what I hope is a smile. "Let's go and meet my maker."

FIVE

WELCOME TO HOOKVILLE says an understated red sign that's so small, it seems apologetic, like whoever hung the sign understood the absurdity of welcoming anyone to a place like this. The crusty sort of blue-green backwater you can only find if you're lost or in desperate need of low-cost real estate. Not quite the end of the universe, but a murky bog in some undesirable corner of the cosmic sewer system. Spiritually similar to the creepshow Idaho mountain towns my father dragged me through the summer after my sophomore year of college. We had a slightly better relationship back then. He told me he wanted to take a road trip, and I wanted to see California. We packed Mom's Honda Odyssey full of supplies, a foam mattress, and a portable shower contraption you could fill with water and hang from a tree. My father loved to say our trip was a walkabout, a vision quest to the Wild West. He told me I could bring as much beer as I wanted. What he didn't tell me was he never intended to take me to California. His real mission was to search for an isolated plot of land where he could bury a boxcar. A fallout-shelter haven big enough for our whole family when the sky finally fell. We ended up driving a bunch of scraggly backwoods roads in Idaho and eastern Washington, winding through strange, haunted villages where the locals evil-eyed us from beneath the brims of their hunting caps. We slept in the van, and the seals around the windows leaked when it rained. We'd wake up damp with woodland mice rifling through our gas station snacks. Those were the longest two weeks of my life—and the last time Henry and I spent any real length of time together.

"We did it," Yivi says, pointing to the Hookville sign.

I wipe liquor sweat off my forehead and hum an affirmative. I've always imagined Arkansas hot, but I never expected this dense, greasy air—like a Rainforest Cafe without the fun plastic animals. It's been drizzling for over an hour, and my arm's getting soaked because I broke the mechanism when I shoved my window down. My face is numb, my gut is bubbling, my heart is stuttering, my ass is stinging, and the vodka is gone. Woe. Is. Me.

Yivi, meanwhile, is chilling. Full-on lounge mode. She's got her Doc Martens propped on the dashboard, and she's swaying her toes to the song where Ariana Grande gets fucked too hard and can't walk straight.

"Pretty funky town," she says, and I nod. Our route is taking us through a ramshackle residential area on the edge of Hookville, and I wish I could say it's better than I expected. But no. Pro-life billboards and trash-bag windows, strip mall churches and potbellies jiggling behind DEATH TO SNOWFLAKES T-shirts. I guess I should feel vindicated, but I'm struggling to feel anything other than depressed.

Before my parents left Illinois, I was holding out hope they might return to the Democratic Party and something approximating political sanity. Maybe it's elitist on my part, but my identity is rooted in the concept of the Northerner. The white-savior emancipator. The purveyor of a more pleasant brand of racism—systemic rather than overt. I'm being glib, but I was raised on the idea that the North won the war, goodness prevailed, and moral superiority was my birthright. Illinois was the homeland of Abraham Lincoln. His solemn face decorated our license plates, and aside from occasional dinner table racism and 1990s-style homophobia, my parents raised me to treat people with respect. My father liked to say he was post-judiced rather than prejudiced, meaning he gave every nonwhite individual a fair shot before he inevitably resorted to racial slurs. At the time, I believed his was an acceptable way to be. My suburb was working-class blue, my teachers were Al Gore libs, and a Bush-Cheney sign was the polite version of a swastika. This was the milieu of my childhood, and I liked it. It seemed righteous then, and it still seems better than the current alternative. Despite the 9/11-truther theories and the covertly anti-Semitic YouTube videos, both my parents voted for Obama twice. They had grown up poor and neither of them finished high school, but they believed in equality and freedom of choice and eating the rich. Then, the housing market crashed, my father became chronically unemployable, and the existential void of their combined disillusionment brought a darkness out of my parents I hadn't seen before.

I didn't understand it, but by that point, I was in college, far too busy making capitalism my personality to directly witness their transformation. I thought, or maybe hoped, it was a phase, but in the summer of 2016, when my father told me Trump was a man of the people, I knew with absolute certainty that Hillary would lose the election. Jenny and Clinton and the rest of my liberal acquaintances called me crazy, but my father was plugged into a very dark mainframe. There was *This American Life*, and there was *that* American life, and the disconnect had become untenable. But that doesn't mean I wasn't furious. When Trump won, I exclusively blamed my father. He cast his vote, and in that moment, Henry Gunderson came to symbolize everything I loathe about this nation.

In the intervening years, though, my fury has cooled to disappointment. Joblessness is a bitch, and my parents' bodies were failing. Any vote for Trump is unforgivable, but I understand marketing, and I recognize the power of a funny, bumbling, orange-faced con man better than most. If the Pillsbury Doughboy could convince Americans pastry comes from tubes, surely a wealthy reality-TV star could convince my father the KKK is just another group of well-meaning fellas in funny hats. I try not to look down my nose at my parents because their lives have been more difficult than mine. In a world where morality is for sale and website charlatans will write anything to increase ad revenue, confusion is a forgivable offense. There's a line, however. A point where a fool becomes complicit in their own foolishness, convincing themselves their con man is a good man because their subconscious ears crave his dog whistles and his liar's promises to resurrect a false social order that made them feel a little bit better and a little bit smarter and a little bit safer than everyone else. It might seem relatively insignificant to anyone who doesn't know them, but my parents' move to Arkansas symbolized a certain amount of dedication to their increasingly problematic ideals. It said, *We know it's wrong, but we're not sorry.*

Now that I'm finally here in their new hometown, however, I'm beginning to understand some things. A few miles back, I saw a woman walking through a forsaken gravel valley lined with used-car lots and boat dealers. The woman looked a lot like my mother, but her hair was a different color, and she was considerably younger. She was also carrying a repurposed Re/Max yard sign that she'd painted over to say I AM GOD'S WARRIOR on one side and JEWS TOOK MY HOUSE on the other. I don't know what to make of that, and I wish she didn't blame the Jewish people, but I suppose I can understand why she's angry. Looking around, I'm angry too.

We're idling at a stoplight in downtown Hookville. To our left is a dirt field, a gray pond, and a dangerously thin man fishing off a sagging dock. To our right is an intermittent strip of aging structures, all topped with the same reddish-brown roofs: Fatso's Burger Fort, Screaming Eagle Grocers, Curl Up & Dye Salon, a freestanding post office, and a boarded-up fire station. Aside from the lone fisherman, the drizzling rain must have chased everyone else indoors.

"Is your dad a big drinker?" Yivi says as the light turns green, and I'm forced to continue.

I scratch a patch of dry skin on my cheek. Yivi has been peppering me with increasingly invasive questions for the past thirty or so minutes, and at this late stage, I lack the energy to defend myself from her curiosity. "Not anymore," I say.

"But he was?"

"Before I was born." The story goes that the last drunken straw was some unserious motorcycle accident. Mom said, *No more*, and he said, *Yes, ma'am*. I find it impossible to believe my father would compromise his selfish desires for anyone, especially Mom, but that's the story.

"So it runs in your family," Yivi says.

I tighten my grip on the steering wheel. "Let's talk about something else."

"I don't mean to wriggle under your skin, babe." Yivi's palms flash like white flags. "We're just running outta road, and I'm trying to figure out why you hate your fam so much."

"Then go ahead and ask me about that."

"Do they give you shit cuz you're queer?"

"My family doesn't know anything about my love life."

"They don't?" Yivi sounds surprised, and surprise is an appropriate reaction. "What about Clinton?" she asks.

"You mean my *roommate*?"

Yivi laughs without cackling, a sign I've genuinely tickled her funny bone. "Holy guacamole, Batbabe."

"I know. It's stupid. But don't worry—I'm about to set the record straight."

Yivi stops laughing. "You're gonna tell your mom?" she asks.

"I've gone toe-to-toe with *Mommy Dearest* before, and I usually emerge unscathed," I say despite the snake pit in my belly. It's not like I hate Mom the way I hate my father. She has a way of annihilating my self-esteem with her Betty Crocker mind tricks, but at present, I'm pretty sure I bother her more than she bothers me. Unfortunately, that's the problem. Even now, my conscience sounds almost exactly like her voice. I've spent a good deal of my life trying to live up to her number one–son expectations. Back when I was acing Scantrons and winning poetry prizes, Mom was my biggest fan. She loved when I graduated summa cum laude from college. She loved when I got a good job and paid off my student loans without help. And she really loved when I sent money home so her and Henry wouldn't lose their house. Then I broke my father's nose at Thanksgiving, and a few things changed.

"You sure you're not a teeny bit scathed?" Yivi asks.

"I'm mostly just angry."

"At your dad? Or your mom?"

"She's supposed to be better than him," I say, and while I know that doesn't answer her question, Yivi doesn't press me for an explanation. I'm grateful. I peek at my phone, and the Google Maps countdown says five more minutes. I squint so the five looks more like an eight. Aside from inertia, there's nothing to stop me from turning this car around—except there is. I don't have a name for this feeling because it's new. Something between duty, resentment, and fear. A lopsided hope drizzled with black bile.

"Babe?" Yivi says after a bit. "You okay?"

"I'm cool," I say, wiping a hot bead of moisture from the corner of my eye.

"Can I tell you something funny?"

"Funny works."

"I'm actually kinda excited to meet your family."

I turn left down a narrow road lined with single-story houses. Irregular boxes clad in peeling beige paint, most of them sporting brand-new Confederate flags and less new Stars and Stripes. We pass a scorched lot, the house burned down to its foundation. Even the trees are dead, but somehow, a Trump flag still dominates the ashen front yard. Blackened yet waving. Like a warning. "How could you possibly be excited?" I ask.

"Cuz you're this completely messed-up, enigmatic basket case, and I get to meet the people who put you in the basket."

I do my own version of Yivi's witch cackle. "*You're* calling *me* an enigma?"

"Wrapped in a friend-murdering douchebag."

My eyes spasm shut, though I can tell Yivi is making a very insensitive joke. "Maybe that's how you really feel," I say, forcing an easygoing tone. "But far as I know, you don't even *have* parents. You just crawled, fully formed, from some black mascara tar pit—a Birthday Cake in one hand and a bottle of Q in the other—but *I'm* the one shrouded in mystery?"

Fattening raindrops smack our windshield, and Yivi scoffs. "If you wanna know some shit, all you've gotta do is ask."

"Are you *kidding*?!"

"I thought we were done with the yelling."

"But I ask all the time!" I say, throwing my hand up so hard, I smack the ceiling.

"No. You don't. Not really."

I catch my reflection in the rearview mirror and frown. I'm pretty sure I've been trying to figure out what Yivi's deal is every day since I met her, but I can't perfectly remember most of those days, so it's possible I'm mistaken.

"What do you wanna know?" Yivi asks.

"How about we start with your parents?"

She inhales sharply and rolls her head around on her shoulders. "Well, my dad's the worst," she says. "And my mom's probably dead."

"*Probably* dead?"

"She left when I was two. Then she came back. Then she left again when I was eight. That's the last I heard from her."

"Oh," I say, and I'm conflicted. That Christmas at Chuck Steinbacher's was the first time my own mom left, but it wasn't the last. I can remember five or six separate leavings, calling her at our aunt's house—*Please, Mom, please come home*—and I wish I hadn't. I wish my brother and I had begged her to take us with her instead. Save us all. Snatch us clear of my unstable father and his maelstrom of bullshit. But we were kids. Eventually, we grew up and moved out, and surprise, surprise, Mom never did leave. After college, I'd still get sporadic calls. Usually Sunday evenings. I'd answer, and Mom would be blubbering, saying this was it, she was finally gone for good. Sometimes I'd stay up all night, hearing her out, cheering her on, but the next time we'd talk, she'd pretend everything was okay.

"It's fine," Yivi says, in a way that doesn't quite convey *fine*. "It was a super long time ago, and I barely remember her except photos. And this dumbass thing." Yivi unzips her fannypack and roots around. I take my eyes off the road as she produces a piece of card stock and unfolds it. A postcard. A faded and wrinkled photo of the St. Louis Gateway Arch. Above the arch, written across the sky, are the words WESTWARD HO! It takes every ounce of my self-control not to laugh, and I still end up coughing boozy spit all over the steering wheel.

"It's not funny, babe," she says. "This crap is the last thing she ever said to me." Yivi flips the card, and the backside shouts LOVE, MOM in jagged, meth-head-style letters. "Crazy bitch."

Yivi returns her postcard to her fannypack, and a realization hits me like a hot-bellied hangover. I battle the urge to grab her and squeeze her bony shoulders until her arachnoid body becomes a part of mine, a gothic appendage I can protect from the world.

"Sorry, Yiv." I cover her hand with my palm because I doubt she would appreciate a bear hug right now. "I'm seriously sorry."

"Like I said: I'm over it."

"Okay." I gaze past her out the passenger window. "We're here, by the way," I say.

"Oh goody," she says, perking up a bit. "I was wondering why we'd stopped."

"I imagined it shittier," Yivi says after an overlong moment of silence. Raindrops plink and plunk onto the hood of our car as the engine settles, and I glare at my parents' house, wondering how a decent place like this could've been so much cheaper than the dump I grew up in.

Yivi drums the side of our empty Sprite bottle. "You wanna go in?"

"Not yet," I say.

Until now, I've only seen photos of this Arkansas house, grainy iPhone 7 renderings Mom sent when they first moved. *Tales from the Crypt: Paula Deen Edition*. Gray woods tangled with undergrowth, garage leaning not-so-slightly to the left, muddy front yard, rust-stained white paint, mildew-streaked windows, and yellowing lace curtains. The final resting place of two people who loathed both life and each other.

In person, though, it doesn't necessarily scream *depressing*. Bigger and cleaner than I imagined. Newer too. The garage may lean a little, but the doublewide door sports a fresh coat of red paint. The surrounding trees are lush and green. The yellow curtains have been replaced with clean white drapes from this century, and the grassless lawn has been swapped for reddish landscaping gravel. As long as I ignore the TRUMP 4 EVER flag nailed to the roof like a billboard for racist aliens, it's basically the nicest house on an otherwise shitshow block.

If I didn't know better, I'd think my father swapped his YouTube videos about interstellar Nazis for motivational TikToks and supply runs to Home Depot, finally making good on all his empty promises to give Mom a decent place to live. In the end, he never actually finished remodeling our house in Franklin

Hole. I had to loan Mom thousands of dollars so she could hire a contractor to get the old place ready to sell, and I'd already been helping pay off their mortgage. Jenny insisted it wasn't my responsibility to support my parents, and I never told Clinton I was sending them money. All in, it cost me like twenty grand. This was after I'd stopped talking to my father, but I still wanted Mom to be happy. I also wanted to absolve myself of the intense shame I experience whenever I'm eating omakase. Now that I'm seeing this shack that they've rehabbed into a respectable residence, though, I'm not positive how I feel. It's possible I'm even angrier. After all of Mom's calls—bitching about Arkansas, moaning about money, whining about my father—I guess I've been expecting her supposedly miserable life to be a tad more miserable than mine.

Yivi slinks out of the car and into the rain. "C'mon, babe. She's probably waiting."

"I know," I say, bracing myself with one final sip of Smirnoff backwash. "That's what I'm afraid of."

Mom answers the door in a ratty Kirkland Signature bathrobe. Her hair is wet, which is fairly on-brand. "Finally," she says, pulling the door aside.

"Hey, Ma." I smile. "It's nice to see you."

"You should've texted to say you were getting close. You surprised me in the middle of my bath."

"Sorry," I say, because it's pointless to mention that she is perpetually bathing, and most of my non-screamy memories of her involve steaming baths.

"Sure you are." Her eyes, cold and blue as my own, crawl across my body. Her lips twitch with disgust. I'm as distasteful as ever, but in a fresh new way. "What in the world are you wearing, Holden?" she asks.

I wince. There it is. The world's whitest white-boy name. "It's a hot new trend," I say, gesturing to her own damp robe. "But I see you've already heard."

"Holden."

"It's a bathrobe from a Motel 6."

"What are those stains?" she asks, sounding at least half-concerned. "Is that *blood*?"

"I fell weird in a gravel parking lot."

"I don't—" Mom pauses. She looks speechless, but she rarely looks that way for long. "What happened to your clothes?"

"We had to leave them."

Mom peers over my shoulder, noticing Yivi. "Who's *we*?"

"Hey there, I'm Yivi," she says, stepping forward with her hand outstretched. "I'm sorry to hear about your husband, but I'm confident we're gonna find him."

Mom stares at Yivi's eager palm, and I stare at Mom. She's always been a battle-axe, and age has only sharpened her edges. My bravery may be buoyed by drunkenness, but both are waning. "What kind of name is that?" Mom asks.

"How's it going, Ma?" I give her my biggest, friendliest grin. "How's tricks?"

"My God, Holden." She shakes her head as Yivi and I step into the house. "It's worse than I ever imagined."

I ignore her theatrics and return to judging my surroundings. The front door opens directly into a living room that smells like fake lavender and Clorox. Instead of a foyer, there's a black rubber doormat and an Ikea side table. A pair of Mom's slip-on Merrell shoes are lying near the door, but my father's matching Merrells are missing in action. I set Dante and Becky's car key on the side table and notice a Precious Moments figurine commemorating my first birthday—psychological warfare.

Mom stalks across the living room, her thin hair dripping onto her shoulders. She takes position near the entryway to the kitchen and folds her arms across her chest, glaring at my mullet like it's a coonskin toupee. "You smell like a bum," she says.

I nod, pleased she said *bum* instead of *drunk*. The dank-dog musk of Dante's seats must be masking our more unsavory odors. "The previous owner of my car had questionable hygiene habits," I say.

"What happened to Clinton's BMW?"

This question catches me sideways. "Clinton?"

"Your *roommate*," she says, as if the word *roommate* is inherently profane.

"Beats me." I swallow a lump of bile crawling up my throat. "Ask Clinton."

"I did."

"What?" It goes without saying that Mom doesn't have a relationship with Clinton. Semi-estranged parents aren't usually friendly with roommates.

"He's been calling me every day for the past two weeks. He even called me this morning, which is more than I can say about you."

Yivi looks worried, and my liquor-logged brain races. Fight or flight or fucked.

"Why?" I ask. "What does he have to do with anything?" Clinton always said he was fine with keeping our relationship secret from my parents and coworkers. He said he didn't mind pretending to be my closest friend if it would help my career. Even when we were young and ostensibly in love, I didn't invite him to my family gatherings, and he didn't invite me to his. This was our understanding, the self-loathing cornerstone of our relationship, and our breaking up shouldn't have changed that.

"He's very upset," Mom says.

I try to speak, to defend myself, but something inside me comes unmoored. My headache pummels my face, and I lean against the wall to make my posture as casual as possible. I mouth a few disconnected words before my vocal cords decide on: "Who gives a shit about Clinton?"

"Is it true, Holden?" Mom asks, her jaw quivering.

I lean harder into the wall, wishing it were a futon in the faraway dark.

"Holden."

I clear my throat and nearly swallow my tongue. "Yes?"

"Is it *true*?"

"Which part?"

Mom's expression shifts from quietly furious to furiously bored. "All of it."

"How about letting me catch my goddamn breath a sec before you blindside me with this Clinton bullshit?" I say, staggering into the kitchen.

"Take off your shoes, Holden."

"I'll mop the mud in a sec."

"What're you doing?"

"I'm thirsty," I say, because I'm stalling. I bend over the sink, sucking tin-flavored water straight from the faucet. While I drink, I spot a lone bottle of Bacardi hiding behind a toaster on the counter. Thank Todd and his whole fucking family. Mom despises drinking, but she loves a rum cake.

"Don't be an animal, Holden," Mom says. "Use a cup." Silverware rattles in the dish drainer as she stomps across the kitchen. "Would you like a cup, Yeezy?"

"Sure," Yivi mutters.

"It's *Yivi*." I dry my lips with the neckline of my robe. "With a *v*."

"Yeefee?"

"I just fucking said it had a *v*."

Yivi throws me a glare that says *Shut up before you make this shit worse*. "Don't worry about it, Mrs. G. My name confuses everybody."

"Don't lie, Yivi." I shake my head. "It only confuses people with racist-ass ears."

"Who's a *racist*?" Mom asks. "Don't you call me a *racist* in my own home."

"I said your *ears* were racist."

Mom opens a cabinet, moving a lot slower than she used to. It's been a long time since we've stood in the same room together, and she looks significantly older. Her irises have faded to a robin's-egg hue, her olive flesh is as dark and shriveled as walnut shells, and the lines around her mouth have deepened to fissures. Mom and I share many features—I like to think of myself as sensually androgynous as a result—and witnessing these physical signifiers of her decline makes me more concerned than ever about the future of my face. Particularly my chin. As a kid, I used to worry Mom might hang herself while I was away at school, but that would be impossible now. Unless she hooked the noose under her ears.

"Did you drive here drunk?" Mom asks. She hands Yivi a Tervis tumbler and advances on my position, her nose working like a bloodhound's. I used to keep a jar of peanut butter in my backpack to disguise my vodka breath, but Mom could still sniff out when I was loaded. I could see it all over her face, even if she rarely said anything. I guess she chose not to shatter her illusion that I was her Great White Hope.

"Just the last couple miles." I blink away a tiny bit of double vision. "It's a long trip."

"Jesus." Mom angles her head skyward as if Christ is nailed to the ceiling. "My own son drinks himself stupid before he can bear to see me."

"Not everything happens because of you," I say, irrationally offended that this woman would still dare to refer to me as *son*. The implied masculinity is one thing, but what bothers me more is the implication of ownership: *You are my son, and therefore my property, and any trauma I inflict upon you is my right.*

Mom's shoves another Tervis tumbler into my face. I grab it and fill it with water. The plastic is foggy and gross, but the water tastes sweeter than rum.

Mom rubs her eyes, and I can tell she's preparing to say something dastardly. Words that will gut me from head to toe. I eye the fifth of Bacardi.

Yivi leans down to inspect a photo hanging off the fridge. "Who are these nice little people?" she asks.

"That's Michael's family," Mom says, momentarily diverted from her conniption. "Holden's brother."

"He's all these kids' daddy?"

"Michael's very prolific," I say, drifting over near Yivi. Next to the photo of my brother's brood, Mom's got an article affixed via magnet to the fridge door: an *Adweek* feature that lists me and Jenny among Advertising's Creative 100. The article is a few years old, but the paper looks fresh, like Mom printed it out in the past few days. Fuck literally all of this.

"Babe," Yivi says. "I can't believe you never told me you had a brother."

"Thought I mentioned it."

"Michael's a very successful businessman over in London," Mom says. "Like Holden used to be."

"You used to live in London?" Yivi asks.

"She means the *successful* part." I grab the Bacardi bottle off the counter and wrestle the cap. Yivi does a super judgmental thing with her lips, and Mom watches me like I'm a particularly tragic cockroach.

"That's not for you, Holden."

I take a long pull of rum and dry my lips with the back of my hand. "What exactly did Double-O Clinton say to you, Ma? Did he tell you about the baseball bat?"

"I want you to put that rum back where you got it."

"Were you saving it?" I guzzle another sizeable sip while I stare her down. When I've had my fill, I sigh with exaggerated commercial satisfaction. "What I need is some clothes," I say. "Where's the hospitality?" I shake my head. "Your kid comes to town, and I can't even get a tour of your place to save my life."

I stomp back into the living room and immediately regret doing so. It's freaky to see the furniture of my youth rearranged inside this happy little house: the matching brown La-Z-Boy recliners, the twenty-year-old Vizio flat-screen with the factory plastic still stuck to its edges, the burnt-orange rug my father knocked me onto the first time I tried to protect Mom, the Ikea bookcases packed with Health Freedom Expo pamphlets, ancient Lemurian textbooks, David Icke psychobabble, and the self-help books Mom reads to supplement her therapeutic bathing regimen. The whole thing is like an incredibly depressing exhibit in a boomer museum, complete with a balding docent offering details like: *This is the chair where they sat and read James Patterson . . . This is hotel art they bought at*

Hobby Lobby . . . This is a Miss Congeniality *VHS that doesn't rewind anymore.*

"You've got a pretty nice house, Mrs. G," Yivi says, reprising her role as peacemaker.

I take another long chug of rum while I reappraise the living room from Yivi's perspective. Frankly, it's a miracle my father worked enough to afford any of this shit, but then, Mom worked too. Checkout clerk at Jewel-Osco so we could get discount produce, cleaning staff at a pediatric dental office so we could get free fillings, circulation desk at the local library so we could snag all the newly released movies before anyone else in town. All those random movies are likely why I've done so well in advertising. I guess I owe Mom a thank-you for that. Too bad she's a giant fucking asshole.

"Holden," Mom says behind me.

"I thought I asked you for some clean fucking clothes."

"Please don't speak to me that way," she says, and it's hilarious coming from a woman who normally uses the word *fuck* like Dunkin' uses sprinkles. Michael told me she joined a church shortly after she and Henry moved down here, but I hadn't realized the Baptists had done such a number on her tongue.

"Babe?" Yivi says, lurking like a frightened child in the kitchen doorway. "Maybe chill?"

"What's the matter, Ma? You don't want to share clothes with a *queer*?"

"Holden!"

"C'mon, Yiv," I say, and Mom flinches as I lumber past her. "Let's raid the closets." I stagger into the hallway off the living room and pause to gather my drunken bearings. There are four identical doors, two on either side of the hall. White doors, white walls, white trim, white hardwood floor. The only pops of color are a series of Navajo sand paintings hanging between the doors, a reminder that my father has always claimed some obscure Native American heritage despite a complete lack of genealogical evidence.

"You've gotta quit it, babe," Yivi says, catching up to me.

"Don't take this the wrong way, Yivi, but has it ever occurred to you that the word *babe* is reserved for assholes you're dating and not assholes you met two weeks ago?"

"Why are you acting like this?" she asks, but I don't care. I'm done pulling punches. Done apologizing for my existence. Done being the obedient, try-hard good boy Mom has always expected me to be.

"I'm not acting like anything." I lurch toward a room on the right and throw my weight against the door. It doesn't budge.

"You're upsetting your mom."

"This is how we show love."

"Don't go in there, Holden." Mom is advancing down the hallway, her bare feet slapping the hardwood. "That room's not ready for you."

I step back, inspecting the door handle, and I notice a small black sticker on the doorjamb. Our old house was covered in these: my father's label-maker labels. Reminders to ALWAYS CLOSE DISHWASHER so we couldn't smell sewage, LEAVE FAN ON so shower mold wouldn't grow, KEEP BLINDS DRAWN so cops and neighbors couldn't spy, and NEVER OPEN GARAGE for reasons I still don't understand. It almost warms my heart to see the controlling weirdo up to his old tricks. SLIDE TO OPEN says the sticker, and I comply, dragging the door sideways and stepping into the darkness.

A wave of stench hits me and rolls into the hall. Stagnant air and elderly carpeting. Microorganisms devouring whatever old men leave behind. My nose twitches as my pickled neurons process a collection of cardboard boxes and lonely furniture. Most of the boxes are piled in the center of the room, and a yellow-stained mattress leans against the wall. The only real evidence that this bedroom belongs to my father is a poster that used to hang over my childhood bed. A faded seventies vector drawing of a man standing at the foot of a mountain. The man is mostly silhouette, but you can tell he's determined to reach the peak. Above him, psychedelic type screams: LONG LIVE THE UNREASONABLE MAN!

"Holden," Mom says from the doorway.

"You guys moving, Ma?"

"No."

"Did you kill him?"

"Stop it."

"Is he *dead*?"

Yivi hovers behind Mom. She looks as befuddled as I feel. The ringing in my ears shrieks louder, rattling my molars. I'm having a tough time seeing out of my left eye again. I walk the perimeter of the room and help myself to a little more Bacardi.

"Give me the alcohol, Holden."

"This is mine now."

"I can't believe this." Mom pushes a few silver hairs out of her face. "I really can't."

"Neither can I," I say, though I'm not precisely sure what it is we both can't believe.

"I won't talk to you until you calm down."

"That's too bad." I shrug. "Because I wasted two whole days of my life driving, and you're chatting up my ex-boyfriend all buddy-buddy, talking behind my back, stealing my goddamn thunder, and now all this—whatever this is—so I wouldn't bet on me calming down anytime soon."

"I don't even know what to say to you," Mom says, and her posture quits. Folds inward.

"Say whatever you want." I widen my stance. "Say I lied about Clinton. Say I'm a circus-freak faggot asshole. Say I got myself fired on purpose. Say *anything*. It's not gonna change the truth, and I'm gonna keep acting exactly like this until you tell me what the fuck is going on!"

Mom trembles. She opens her mouth. Closes it. She glances sidelong at Yivi, as if they're suddenly on the same team. And maybe they are. Maybe it's me against everybody. Unreasonable Man but not even a man.

"I think you need help, Holden."

"What I need is clothes," I say, yanking at my robe and stumbling sideways. I swallow an upsurge of bile, and Yivi's eyes shine. Her mouth droops. A sad-girl face on a space-alien body. And I hate it. I want to fix her face almost as much as I want Jenny back, and I want Jenny back almost as much as I want my head to quit buzzing. The pain. Sharp and hot where Clinton did whatever he did. *Battered my brains* sounds silly when I think the words. Silly and stupid and scary. I'm a little worried I'm finally dying, but I refuse to die in this robe.

"Clothes." I wobble around, a slow pirouette. There's a closet on the far wall. Two mirrored door panels. I rush across the room and toss the sliding door aside. Empty.

"There's stuff in the boxes," Mom says, pointing.

I peer at the cardboard pile in the center of the room. Secrets, secrets. I fall to my knees and rip open a box. Knickknacks and nonsense. I knock it aside with my rum bottle and tear open another. Jackpot.

"Holden."

I grab a stack of neatly folded clothes and toss them onto the ragged beige carpet. A menagerie of T-shirts, cargo shorts, and ratty jeans. My father is an XXL beast, way wider than me, but a drawstring will help.

"Listen to me, Holden."

I choose a pair of black gym shorts and an oversized black T-shirt bearing the CARPENTER'S LOCAL #1 logo. I roll onto my sliced-up ass and pull the shorts up under my robe.

"I know you're upset."

I peel off my robe and toss the bloodstained terry cloth into the corner. Then I spot something awful. A landslide of personal effects spilling out of the knickknack box and, most offensively, a photo of my father. He and Mom together and smiling. Two lovebirds seated in an unfamiliar room. Mom is wearing a blue ski-vest over a sweater, my father a black silk button-up printed with illustrations of constellations. A star-gazing dreamer before the internet turned his brain into unvaccinated mashed potatoes.

"Where is he?" I whisper to Mom, my eyes still stuck to the photo. He's bald these days, but here, his curls are long and red. His eyes blue and warm. His nose upturned and proud.

I swivel my head toward the mirrored closet door, and there I am: a hunched and haunted body. I shiver to witness the moon-bleached gut folding over the thighs, the wild hair sticking to the neck, the glassy eyes sinking into the brow, the mottled cheeks dangling off the jaw, the piggish nose gleaming like a hot wet growth. The man Jenny and Clinton knew—the liar, the winner, the coward—would have averted his gaze at this pathetic sight. But not me. I'm smiling, delighted, and the creature in the mirror looks pretty goddamn happy too. Because we know the truth. I'm not the man in the photo, and I'll never be any kind of man after this. I'm free.

A gaunt hand closes around my bare shoulder. "Babe," someone says, and I flinch. I lurch away from the bony fingers. I lash out with my elbow.

"DON'T TOUCH IT!" I shout.

"WHAT THE FUCK, BABE!" Yivi says as she tumbles to the carpet.

"Jesus Christ, Holden," Mom says.

"I'm not Holden," I mutter, and in the mirror, the pale thing is shaking.

"Are you alright?" Mom bends to help Yivi to her feet.

I rip my attention away from the mirror and stand with my father clenched in my fists. "My name isn't *Holden*."

"What in the world are you talking about?"

"I guess Clinton didn't tell you about that, huh?" I toss my throbbing head back and unleash a real-life witch cackle. "I'm my own thing now. You don't own me. No one does. I got rid of it all, and if you don't like who I am anymore, then you officially hate the real me."

"This is way beyond nuts," Yivi says, fixing her robe.

"No, Yivi. It's honest."

"You can't keep doing this," Mom says quietly. "You can't keep hurting people."

My knees rattle, and my brain sloshes between my ears. "Hurting *who*?" I ask.

"I understand what happened between you and Henry. And I understand why. But there's no excuse for what you did to poor Clinton."

I strangle my father's picture in my fists. The wooden frame creaks. I look to Yivi for backup, but she's staring at the floor. "What did Clinton say to you?" I ask.

"You need help," Mom says. "It's been a long, long time since you've acted like yourself, but I couldn't reach you. First, you wouldn't talk to your father. Then you'd barely talk to me."

"That's not true."

"I've *tried* to call you. To reach you. But whenever we talk, you never sound like yourself."

I clamp my hands over my ears. "Stop it."

"Everything makes you angry. And I've been so—so afraid to make you worse, I couldn't even tell you about your father."

"My father," I say, and I remember the room. The boxes. The yellow mattress against the wall. "Where the fuck is my father?"

"Holden."

"Tell me where he went."

"Calm down."

"Tell me."

"You're upset." Mom clasps her vein-streaked hands. "You're in pain." She looks above me, below me, through me, but she won't look *at* me.

"I'm fucking fine, Mom."

"You're not."

I peer down at my father's grinning face. "Just tell me where he is."

"He's—" Mom hesitates. "I don't know where he is."

"How the fuck is that possible?"

"He left a very long time ago."

The room wobbles on its axis, and I stumble against the mirror. I rest my shoulder on the cold glass, sucking air through my tightening windpipe. "How long?" I ask.

"A year," Mom says, staring at the floor. "Close to two."

"TWO *YEARS*?!"

"Please, babe." Yivi sounds scared. "Please relax."

"YOU DIDN'T TELL ME?!" I raise my voice to maximum, though it's hard to shout with my throat constricting. "FOR TWO FUCKING YEARS, YOU DIDN'T TELL ME?!" I slam my fist against the mirror.

"Stop." Mom is crying now. Full-on. Really going for it like she's been doing since the nineties when she'd lie in bed with the blinds drawn, whimpering, telling me again and again that she just wanted to die.

"THEN WHY AM I EVEN HERE?!"

"You're here because I was worried."

I try to shout again, but this time my voice comes out a whisper: "What?"

"I want to help you," Mom says, not loudly but clearly. "Clinton called me, and he said you'd—you'd lost it. You'd completely disappeared. I'm your mother, Holden. I was worried. The police have also been calling, and I had no way to find you. I tried to get in touch with Jenny, some of the people at your job, and they told me what happened, and I—I needed a way to make you come to me."

"You lied."

"I know she was your best friend."

"You *lied* to me."

"I know how much it hurts to lose a friend like that."

"You're a fucking liar." I'm stunned. Empty. "Like everyone else," I say, but I can't hear her response. A waterfall roars past my ears, and I slide along the mirror. I wonder what an aneurism sounds like. I jerk my head sideways and retch.

"Holden," Mom says, and she shouldn't have said it.

I hurl my father's photo over her shuddering shoulder, and it explodes against the opposite wall. "C'mon, Yiv," I say, turning my back on my family for what I swear is the last time. "We've got better places to be."

SIX

Rain punishes our windshield, and the sky through the treetops is the deepest, purplest dark. My phone is nearly deceased, and I am navigating by instinct because my memory is too busy replaying shit with Mom. That hypocritical, manipulative bitch. Crying at me while I finished dressing, grabbing me as I walked out the door, screaming at our car from the porch—the exact same kind of crazy-type scene she'd pull with my father in Franklin Hole, outbursts that earned me sideways looks from the kids at school, judgmental glances like the one Yivi is currently shooting me out of the razor-blade corners of her eyes, as if she's the Doctor fucking Phil of healthy interpersonal relationships.

Buzz, buzz, buzzzzzz. My phone is ringing again, obviously, but I let that noise go to voicemail. I don't care if it's Todd himself calling; I'm not in the mood for a chat.

"Babe?"

"Not right now." I'm not in the mood for Yivi's sad-girl nonsense either. She's supposed to be on my side, and I swear to shit, if she tries to send me on another guilt trip, her skinny little garbage-goth ass is walking back to Chicago.

Yivi thrusts the glowing screen into my face. The caller ID reads Brother Michael, and I'm surprised. It's an extremely rare treat to get a call from jolly old London town.

"Maybe you should answer?" she says.

I snatch my iPhone and toss it into the backseat. "Maybe you should climb outta my dick hole before you get your face stuck."

"What the fuck is wrong with you?"

"I'm drunk," I say, swigging from the Bacardi bottle I'm keeping wedged between my legs. I can barely see the road, and my steering is unreliable at best. I have no clue where we're going, but there's no way we're making it back to society tonight. Or ever. It's not like I could actually beat a case or land a new job in my condition, and I'm fresh out of funds for food and fun and futons.

"I *know* you're drunk."

"Don't say it like it's a bad thing."

"It's not safe to drive when you're like this."

"It's not safe to dodge gunshots either, but today's turning out to be a very special occasion, and frankly, I'm exceedingly disappointed you didn't see all this ridiculous horseshit coming in your dreams."

"Fucking *fuck*, man." Yivi grabs her hair, squeezing fistfuls of damp curls. She snagged another of my father's giant T-shirts on the way out of Mom's house, a bright yellow Panama Jack situation that matches her fannypack, and she's wearing it as a dress. It's a better outfit than mine, which is slightly annoying. "I can't believe we drove all the way down here just so you could lose your entire mind," she says.

"Well boo-bunny-hoo, Yiv. I sure am sorry I got you caught up in my mom's scheme to turn me over to the cops. Maybe you can find it in your shriveled demon heart to forgive me since I'm the only schmucky jagoff in the whole wide world who's generous enough to cover your daily Taco Bell requirements."

I expect Yivi to shout, to give me what I deserve, but instead she grabs my thigh. "Please, babe. Just chill. You're scaring me."

I gun the engine up a steep and slippery hillside. The Corolla is vibrating like *The Thing*. It's possible that the engine is deep-throating pistons, but that could also be the noise in my throbbing brain. "Keep your eye out for a bar," I say.

"We should pull over."

I chuckle and roll my highly impaired eyes. "What's the worst that could happen?"

Yivi growls. She shakes her fists around. "I need you to stop being this way."

"I really don't understand why *you're* so pissed," I say. All this time, I've thought Yivi was some hardcore, drug-dealing wild child—an unreasonable chick hell-bent on living her anti-capitalist truth—but here she is treating me like a disease.

"You don't understand *anything* about *anything*," she says.

"I thought you liked me for who I am."

"I don't even know who that is."

"Excuse me?"

"You threw a picture frame at your own mom's head, and now you're driving like a total drunken psycho."

"I didn't throw the picture at *her*," I say.

"What about Clinton?"

"Don't talk to me about Clinton."

"Your mom said you hurt him."

At this, I explode: "JESUS FUCKING CHRIST, YIVI!"

"Stop."

"I DIDN'T HURT *HIM*!" I roar. "CLINTON BASHED MY FUCKING SKULL IN WITH A FUCKING BASEBALL BAT

BECAUSE I DIDN'T WANNA BE HIS FUCKING BOYFRIEND ANYMORE!"

"I DON'T CARE!" Yivi roars back. "I DON'T EVEN CARE WHAT YOU SAY CUZ I DON'T BELIEVE YOU."

"BUT IT'S *ME*, YIVI! IT'S *ME*! YOU KNOW *ME*!"

"NO! I DON'T!"

I punch the gas harder. I would love to keep screaming, but my lungs are failing, and my brain is probably bleeding. Also, I give up. I thought Yivi was different, but nobody cares what's real. Nobody cares about the fakers and the creeps, the boyfriends and the fathers. My biggest, saddest truth is I'd love to keep playing the liar. I'd love to tell Mom I'm sorry. To go back to Chicago, curl up in Clinton's king-sized Casper, soar off to sleep with *Seinfeld* streaming, and wake up freshly hungover for work. But that's all over now. It's been ending for a while, but I didn't realize it for sure until I beat my knuckles bloody on Jenny's hotel door. I thought she was fine, I really did, but she wasn't, and neither was I. I'd convinced myself that I was rich, cool, winning. But I was dying. We both were. We all are. And how could Yivi understand that? How could Mom? That woman couldn't even lie when it was in everybody's best interest. She'd be terrifying baby Michael, saying we were gonna lose our house, starve to death, die under a bridge downtown, and I used to think:

Can't you keep that shit to yourself?

Can't you wait till he's older?

Can't you just pretend?

"Please, babe, please slow down," Yivi says as I blow another pointless stoplight.

"Why?" I say, but I'm still dwelling on Mom. All the times she said she hated Arkansas, said she missed me, said she wished she could move back to Illinois. And the guilt I felt. Imagining her trapped down here with that crazy old man. Suffering. But it was me doing the suffering. Me without a mom. And now this. She stayed down here for two years without him. Two whole *years*! If she was genuinely worried, then why the fuck didn't she come visit me?

"It's not safe to drive like this," Yivi says.

"I've got places to be."

"But where we gonna go, babe?" Yivi asks, calmly and slowly. "We don't even have money for gas."

I gnaw my lip as I yank the car to the left, narrowly avoiding a pair of headlights that comes out of nowhere. "You know what? You're right," I say, twisting around to search for my phone. "Do me a hot little favor and grab the wheel for a sec?"

"Are you completely fucking psycho right now?" Yivi says as she crawls over my ass and grabs the steering wheel. I fumble around, raking my fingers through the greasy garbage spoiling Dante's crumb-covered backseat until my fist closes around my iPhone. Hip-hip-hallelujah. I thump back into my chair, jostling Yivi out of position. She falls back into her own seat with a grunt.

"Found it," I say, unlocking my phone with one hand while I keep us in the general vicinity of this not-quite-empty Arkansas highway with the other. I google CHASE BANK CUSTOMER SERVICE and call the number. Then I press 1 a few times and tell a cheerful robot my debit card was stolen.

"What are you doing?" Yivi asks, but I ignore her.

The robot puts me on hold, and while I wait, I imagine Dante and Becky giving all my hard-earned blood money to their freakazoid father. Two young fools, trapped forever in the downward spiral of poverty dreams and misplaced hope, full-fuck fated to grow up sad and weird and angry, their minds festering until, thirty years from now, they feel a great sense of purpose in helping to elect yet another genocidal nepo-populist promising a return to the American economic greatness of the 2020s. There is no way out of this cycle. The lies reign, and the truth is all but extinct. If the family is the cradle of the world's misinformation, then America is the abusive parent who imbues that young, impressionable misinformation with the drive to dominate its peers. Survival of the cruelest, the sickest, the try-hardest alternative facts. In other words, Dante and Becky are way beyond screwed. Their chances are slim, and any hope my misguided cash infusion might provide only sets them up for a more profound and inevitable letdown. It's a mercy to take back this money, and I feel a burst of altruistic joy when the robot says it has taken care of my security issue. It asks if I need to update my address to receive a new card, but I hang up because I don't know where I'll be tomorrow.

"You're like one of the top ten shittiest people on the planet," Yivi says.

"Pretty sure there's more than ten people in Congress." I grin at Yivi, but she's crying again. "What's wrong?" I ask. "Aren't you concerned about our financial future?"

"I—" Yivi chokes out a sob. "I don't wanna do this anymore."

"Do what? *Drive?* I can pull over in a bit if you really want. It's not that big of a deal."

Yivi's skeletal fingers tremble as she unzips her fannypack. She pops two red Qs and shuts her eyes, sucking quick, shallow breaths.

"Don't clam up on me, cupcake," I say.

"Fuck you," Yivi says. "And fuck you for fucking my life up even worse."

I laugh on accident and regret it immediately. "Yivi—"

"Stop." She heaves a gargantuan sigh. "I don't even wanna hear it."

"You don't want to hear *what*? That my mom's a phony-ass lying bitch?"

"Your mom cares about you, dipshit. She *worries* and she *cares*, and you should really quit taking people for granted cuz literally the *only* reason I'm even here with you right now is I thought you'd end up dead if I didn't get into this car."

"Well, Yivi," I say, "that's a pretty dumb reason."

She wipes her tears on her baggy yellow sleeve. "I know."

"You clearly care way too much about someone who doesn't share your feelings."

"What do you mean?"

"It's not my fault you fell in love with a monster."

Her mouth drops open, and for an instant, I worry she might punch me directly in the nose. Instead she says, "Stop the car."

"Yivi."

"Stop the car right now."

"Wait—" I say, the start of a sentence that might mutate into a full-hearted apology.

"I SAID STOP THE FUCKING CAR!"

I check left and right, and twin ditches flank either side of the road. "But there's nowhere to pull over."

"STOP"—she grabs her door handle—"OR I SWEAR I'LL JUMP."

"Fine." I stomp the brakes, fishtailing as Yivi screams and continues screaming when we don't even crash into a ditch.

"I can't take it," she says, once she's regained her voice. "I can't take your giant ego and your violent mood swings and your total disregard for who I am and what I want. You were right:

I *should've* stayed in Missouri. I *should've* let you self-destruct by yourself. But I thought this trip would be fun. I thought you were this super interesting person who saw the world in this completely fascinating way, but you're nothing but a total scumbag fraud pretending you're cool and tragic and damaged while *you* damage everybody who's stupid enough to give a shit about you. After everything I've seen you do, I don't believe your ex-boyfriend was abusive, I don't believe your dad is as bad as you say, and I'm not even sure I believe you didn't mean to kill your friend. And that means you've got no excuse for the shit you've put me through. You're lucky. You've lived a *completely* standard life, and your only *real* problem is that you're a crazy loser alcoholic with a massive emotional malfunction, and I can't believe—" Yivi stops, fighting to catch her breath.

I blink and sip more drink, attempting to subdue my excuse-making tongue as my head warbles. Luckily, an angry driver behind us slams their horn. "What can't you believe?" I ask when the honking stops and the car flies around us.

Yivi presses her mouth into a thin dark line.

"What can't you believe?" I ask again.

She scoffs. A hateful sound. "Fuck this." She opens her door. "I'm done. See you never."

"Stop." I grab her wrist.

"Let *go*," Yivi says, when she realizes she can't drag 180 pounds of ungendered sentient worm food out of the car. "JUST LET ME FUCKING GO!"

"I'm not letting you wander out here all alone."

"FUCK *OFF*!" Yivi shouts, digging a trio of gashes down my wrist with her nails. I release her arm, and Yivi bolts into the downpour, dashing straight through the beam of the Corolla's headlights before tumbling, face-first, onto the pavement.

I fumble with the door latch, my blood-slick hands sliding across the lock. After a few incredibly long seconds, I kick open the door and lurch into the road. When I reach Yivi, she's sprawled face-down, sobbing with her forehead buried in the sleeves of my father's Panama Jack T-shirt.

"Hey," I say, placing my bloody palm on her shoulder.

She jerks away from my hand and rolls onto her back. "Don't touch me," she says as I inspect her furious face for injury and find she's fine.

"We need to get off this road before we're clocked by an underpaid trucker."

The rain rinses away Yivi's Beetlejuicy cosmetics, revealing a surprising softness that risks breaking the last untainted piece of my heart. "Who the fuck even cares?" she asks.

"I do, Yivi—so let's please make our way over to the shoulder."

"Stop being nice to me."

"I'm just being realistic."

"God," Yivi groans. "You literally *never* say the right thing."

"Fair enough. Now c'mon." I squat above Yivi and grab her biceps. "Don't make me manhandle you because then I'm misgendering myself."

"Quit it." Yivi knocks away my arms and clambers to her feet. A cinematic bolt of lightning erupts overhead, illuminating her eyes. I've inspired a great deal of distaste in my life, but I've never been read the way she's reading. "The worst part is I can't even be totally mad at you cuz it's, like, mostly my fault," she says.

"What is?" I ask.

"Deciding it wasn't a totally shitty idea to be your friend."

I pause, frozen in the subzero sincerity of her words. Because she's right. We're not the same. She's sold some drugs and seen some shit, but she can't go where I'm going. She can't face what I need to face. "What made you decide to do that?" I ask, lowering my voice.

"I'm a fucking idiot." Yivi looks off into the dark. "And you're a lot less horrible than you're trying to be."

"I'm not trying to be *horrible*, Yiv. I'm trying to be *honest*."

"Maybe that's the same fucking thing."

"I hope not," I say as I spot another pair of headlights hurtling toward us. I point at the Corolla. "Either way, you should take the car."

"I don't need it."

"Maybe you don't. But I'm not letting you tramp off into the woods knowing Big Gravy could be out there looking for you. I've got enough ugly crap on my conscience."

A sad smile crests her lips. "So this is it?"

"I thought that's what you wanted."

A huge blue F-150 honks politely as it rumbles past us and thunders up the road. I'm half expecting Yivi to say something important or profound, but she doesn't. Instead, she shuffles back to our car.

I limp into the tall grass growing up from the roadside ditch. The engine whines as Yivi double-starts the Corolla, but eventually, the tires begin to roll. She accelerates, and I hear something pop. In the glow of her taillights, I spot Yivi's trusty pill bottle, crushed by one of the tires. I wave to her as I grab the bottle, but she doesn't see me, and maybe it's for the best. Yivi's still got a chance to change her life, and I'm in the mood to try some questionable drugs.

SEVEN

I'm two steps inside the door at Uncle Slaton's Christmas Club, and this joint is already shaping up to be my kind of liquor locker. After spending the past several hours suicide-strutting down the centers of rain-soaked Arkansas side streets, basking in the easy-peasy pleasure of Yivi's Q pills, I'm extremely ready for a drink, and this festive dive will do. I've always been a holly jolly Christmas fan—everything but the Jesus and family parts—and I love a bar with a theme. Twinkling red and white lights crisscross the ceiling, shiny wrapping paper envelops the tabletops, a big fat Tannenbaum glows near the bathrooms, an old-school jukebox blares "Blue Christmas," and an out-of-place mechanical bull that isn't actually a bull or even a reindeer hogs the corner—a large metal warthog or something? A mechanical Yule pig?

I watch the Yule pig whip and gyrate, jostling a surprisingly sexy rider who's drawing half-hearted cheers from a boring group of twentysomething country bros who seem to be Uncle Slaton's only other customers. Not my ideal crowd, but who cares. The last thing I need is another friend.

I head to the bar. The carpeted floor buzzes beneath the soles of my waterlogged Balenciagas, like I'm trudging through twelve inches of unseasonable snowfall, and suddenly everything feels slow. Possibly a side effect of the Q, but more likely another fun symptom of my brain damage. Regardless, I'm loving the way this slow-motion vibe is warping Elvis's voice.

"You alright there, pal?" asks another voice.

I slide onto a barstool and nod at a black-bearded bartender dressed as Santa Claus. "I'll have a rum and Coke with the darkest, spiciest rum you've got," I say.

"Coming up," Blackbeard Santa says, lingering to inspect my sodden clothes. "Want a towel to dry your head?"

"Yeah, man. Thanks. A towel would be tight."

Blackbeard Santa adjusts his red hat. "I'll see what we can do." He limps away to prepare my drink. I stare intently as he pours—pleased to see he plays fast and loose with the rum-to-Coke ratio—and I barely notice when the sexy individual who was riding the Yule pig hops onto the stool next to mine.

"Hi," they say.

"Howdy," I reply, because this is Arkansas.

"You stole my seat," they say, gesturing at the only thing keeping me off the floor.

"You stole my—" I start, but stop myself before I say *heart*.

"Your . . . *what*?"

"Never mind." I wave away my stupidity. "Cool pig riding you did."

The Yule-pig rider cocks their head, and holy shit, they are very fucking adorable. Shoulder-length strawberry hair, pinkish freckled cheeks, soft yet powerful jaw. I correct my posture and neutralize my expression, attempting to look slightly less drug-addled as they give me a once-over. I normally don't like this sensation—the oozing alien feeling I get whenever I'm inspected by people more attractive than me—but this time, I'm at peace with it.

"Here's a rag," Blackbeard Santa says. He delivers my rum and Coke and waves a ratty dish towel in my face. I take it and mop my hair.

"Holy shit, bud," the Yule-pig rider says as I toss the towel onto the bar.

"What?" I ask.

"I *knew* I recognized you!"

I swallow half my drink and search for an escape route. "You must be thinking of someone else."

"Definitely not." Their pretty mouth spreads into a smile. "You're Holden, aren't you?"

"That's not my name," I say, beginning to recognize the Yule-pig rider's eager face.

"Sure it is," he says. "I'd know you anywhere. You were my first ever boss in advertising."

Becoming known is my least favorite part of existence, but it's true. I do know this guy: Fingerbone Smite. He was my intern five or six years ago, back when I was Holden, a twenty-five-year-old copywriter hotshot, and he was Fing, a slightly younger hot dog who had a lot more raw talent than our dipshit creative directors gave him credit for.

"Damn, bud," Fing says after saying countless other things that I definitely wasn't listening to. "It's crazy unreal to see you."

"I don't disagree."

"What the heck are you doing here?" Fing asks, signaling the bartender for a beer.

I chug my drink and slide the empty glass toward Blackbeard

Santa. "I'll take a double this time." I turn my attention back to Fing. "I'm drinking myself to death. You should try it."

He laughs and punches my thigh. "It's good to see you've still got the jokes."

"That's why they paid me the medium bucks." I grin with all my teeth, allowing my knee to graze his. It might be the twinkling lights or the headache waltzing with my amygdala, but I swear my old intern's face is a little friendlier than friendly tonight. "How about you, Mister Fingerbone?" I ask. "What the fuck are you doing down here in Middle of Nowhere, Arkansas?"

"Well," Fing says, blinking. "I live here, bud."

I chew this information while chewing the inside of my cheek. My mental hard drive doesn't contain much biographical data on Fingerbone—I knew him for like four months before he turned down a full-time gig and disappeared—but I always figured that he was a queer city dweller like me. He used to have a raging case of twink face, which was never my jam, but the twink parts have gone twunk. If I squint, he looks a bit like a redheaded Sigourney Weaver, which is hot. Harry Dean Stanton would be preferable, but either way, I've always wanted to be ass-fucked by a crewmember of the Nostromo. "Really?" I ask. "On purpose?"

Fing laughs. "I grew up two towns over, and I wanted to be closer to my folks."

"Wow," I say, and I'm jealous. I suppose if my father promised to get a full-scale lobotomy, then it might be nice to live near him.

"What can I say?" Fing shrugs his shapely shoulders. "I feel like me when I'm home."

I nod like I understand. I myself have never known such a place, but sometimes I've found substitutes. The futon next to

Yivi's. Or the desk next to Jenny's. Or the computer chair next to my father's while he casually explained how the souls of women can sometimes reincarnate into the bodies of men. "Are you still writing copy?" I ask.

Fing nods. "I'm freelancing in-house for Walmart, which is chill. They're over in Bentonville, so I drive in for the meetings."

"That's great, man. I hope you're taking those town-killing corporate leeches for all they're worth."

"I'm just happy they're happy." Fing sips his beer. "But hey, didn't I see the other day that you got promoted to like a group-level creative director?"

"LinkedIn provides an essential service," I say.

"Congrats, bud. That's huge."

"I can't even begin to tell you how excited I was."

"And I bet Jenny's psyched too. How's she doing, by the way?"

"Oh," I say. I was hoping he'd forgotten she existed, but Jenny is fairly unforgettable.

"Y'all still working together?"

"Of course," I say, and it's not really a lie. Neither Jenny nor I are currently employed, but our friendship is not the kind that death can tear asunder. That might sound ridiculous to the uninitiated, but advertising creative partners share a sacred bond. United, we possessed real vision, and our potential transcended space and time. That promotion Fing mentioned was just the beginning. I'd been going behind our boss JZ's back, talking to the holding-company goons in France, and I had it all situated. We were guaranteed to win that pitch in Cleveland, and after that, Jenny and I were going global.

"Y'all were always such a badass team," Fing says.

"Are those your friends over there?" I ask, gesturing toward the bros who keep glancing our way. There's six of them, all seated at a pair of tables near the mechanical Yule pig.

"Yeah, bud. That's my crew. This is sorta our spot."

"I thought you said I stole your seat."

"That was a line." Fing blushes, and it's cute. "I had this feeling I recognized you, and I wanted to give myself a closer look."

"Ah," I say, disappointed. I was hoping my animal magnetism had lured him over.

"What's *really* going on with you, though?" Fing asks. "I've been racking my brain, and the only reason I can figure you're sitting here in this particular bar on a Sunday night is you're here to murder me."

"You got me, Fing. I'm the T-1000."

"The *what*?"

"Don't worry about it," I say. My memory's still shot, but I vaguely recall taking it personally when Fing told me he didn't want to stay on at the company. He'd written some pretty decent headlines that summer, and a copywriter who can spell over 50 percent of their words correctly is an extremely rare thing. I remember arguing with Jenny because she didn't want to convince Fing to stay. It was her opinion that more talent meant more competition, and more competition meant a slower career trajectory for dynamic young professionals like us. That might sound petty and ungenerous, but I don't blame her. Advertising is a business of phonies and fools, the only industry where dishonesty is called *creativity*, and once you realize the game is entirely pointless, only an idiot wouldn't play to win.

"But seriously." Fing scratches the underside of his ear. "Why're you here?"

"You really want to know?" I ask, avoiding Fing's eyes while I massage the spongy spot in my skull. "This is probably an over-share, but the truth is my mom tricked me into driving to Arkansas because I lost my job and broke up with my boyfriend, and she's worried I'm having a nervous breakdown."

Fing's face strikes a variety of poses as he politely processes my news. "How'd you lose your job?" he asks, and I don't blame him. If I heard somebody say what I just said, I'd focus on the easy part too.

"Do you remember JZ Sugar?" I ask.

"The big bad boss man," Fing says.

"I essentially got myself fired for assaulting him in a client meeting."

Fing misses his mouth with his glass, and beer foam splashes onto his shirt. "Is that a joke?"

"We were in Cleveland for a pitch, and JZ was talking his usual shit, and I lost it."

"Lost it?"

"I grabbed a red gel pen off a conference table and tried to stab him in the neck."

Fing's mouth twitches, but before he can ask any follow-up questions, Blackbeard Santa materializes with our next round of drinks. Fing takes his fresh pint, and I accept my supersized rum and Coke with the quiet glee of a hungover child on Christmas morning.

"It honestly sounds crazier than it was," I continue, after Blackbeard Santa departs. "I didn't even break skin, and afterward, I actually felt pretty calm."

"Right," Fing says gently, as if he's talking to Hannibal Lecter. "But they fired you?"

"Basically, yeah. They wouldn't even let me fly back to Chicago on the agency's dime, so I took a Megabus home. You know they don't even ask you for an ID when you ride those things?"

Fing sips his beer, studying me over the rim of his glass like he doesn't believe my story. But that's fine. It feels good to tell someone who knows all the characters.

"Anyway," I say after chugging the majority of my drink, "that was two whole weeks ago, and I'm doing a lot better now."

"You're not, like, messing with me, are you?" Fing asks.

"I'd never do that without your consent."

"For sure, Holden." Fing's eyes flick toward the drink wobbling in my hand. "And no offense, but you might want to consider slowing down with the boozing."

"You're sweet," I say, leaning over and kissing his cheek. It's a nice kiss, nice enough that he barely recoils and only nearly falls off his stool. "I'm afraid I need to inform you, though, that my name isn't Holden anymore. I haven't decided on a new name yet, but you can call me Nobody Gunderson if you'd like."

"You're not going by *Holden*?" Fing glances back at his gaggle of friends as if he needs saving. A friend, however, is a poor excuse for a savior. For years, I thought Jenny was saving me from myself. I assumed she had my back. That day at Chili's, the day I told her I was genderqueer, was also the day our agency's HR department mandated that everyone in the company add pronouns to our email signatures. This was a while after Fing had left, but it was still a long time ago. JZ was really starting to notice Jenny and me, and Trump had only been in office for a few miserable years. I was angry about so many things, and I'd been growing increasingly uncomfortable with my false status as a man. I wasn't raised on TikTok, and I didn't have the language to understand my gender for most of my life, but I remember sitting in front of my laptop, typing HE/HIM, HE/THEY, FUCK/YOU, and then deleting my signature altogether. It was a rare slow day at the office, so I made Jenny leave early. We went to Chili's. We ordered ribs. I started talking. She listened and drank, and when I was finished, she calmly explained that, while she saw where I was coming from, and she loved me for who I was, I probably needed to keep my cute new identity to myself. That's a direct quote—*cute new identity*—and while I think she was trying to make a joke, it hurt. Jenny used to proudly claim that she would do anything to succeed, and I internalized that perspective as well. As much as it sucked, it didn't seem strange when she made me promise not to tell our coworkers who I really was. I'd been hiding my relationship with Clinton from almost everyone, and I knew she was right. A man and a woman make a good team, but a queer and a woman are an oddity. Our clients wanted to sleep with Jenny, and they wanted to get drunk with me. This was a big part of our brand, our angle, our unique selling proposition, and Jenny was worried I'd fuck everything up.

"By the way," I say, because I can tell Fing is tremendously ready for this interaction to end. "What's the deal with that Yule pig you were riding?"

"The *what*?"

"The big metal boar-thing over there?"

"That's a mechanical razorback."

"Like the football team," I say, momentarily glad that I used to watch ESPN as research for my role as Cishet White Man.

"Right."

"Sick." I leap off my stool and teeter toward the big metal animal. "I'm gonna go ride it."

"You sure this is safe to do right now, bud?" Fing says to my ass cheeks as I wiggle onto the razorback Yule pig.

I wrap my free hand around a leather handle near the base of the razorback's head. The metal is cold against my thighs, and it occurs to me that I'm going commando. I tug down the bottom hems of my shorts. "How do I make this thing go?" I ask.

Fing walks with wooden strides to a control panel on the wall. "I can turn it on if you really want," he says.

"Turn me on, baby!" I holler, drawing a few confused looks from Fing's friends. I generally try to contain my flamboyancy, especially when I'm in the company of potential hostiles, but what have I got to lose. "Turn me on! Turn me on! Turn me on!"

And he does. The razorback rumbles to life.

"HEY! STOP! YOU CAN'T DRINK UP THERE!" Blackbeard Santa shouts.

"YIPPEE-KI-YAY, MOTHERFUCKERS!" I scream as the razorback seesaws with slow and steady thrusts.

"Hold on, Holden," Fing says, and while I'm pissed to hear that name after I shared my truth, I'm flattered he cares enough to give me pointers.

"Do your worst, pig," I whisper, when the razorback bucks its first real buck. I tighten my grip on the cracked leather reins, whipping forward, then back, then side to side. I lean into each defiant pulse, anticipating the monster's movements. My liquor-numb body is buzzing with Q, and my brain is throbbing in a much more pleasant way than usual. I am Bitch Cassidy taming the Sundance Pig. I squeeze my bare calves tighter against its sides. Rum sloshes onto my father's shirt and splashes into my eyes. I lose track of Fing, but I can feel him watching, seeing me for what I am. My power, my prowess, my down-but-never-out determination.

"Is that all you've got?" I ask as the beast kicks harder, moving with violence, enraged by my tenacity. My indomitable will. Winning through determination, as usual. The only piece of worthwhile career advice I ever got from my father was *Success is moving from fuckup to fuckup with enthusiasm*. And boy have I fucked shit up.

"Careful, Holden!" Fing shouts from somewhere far away.

I crane my head, searching for my old intern's beautiful face, but I'm lost. The razorback leaps toward the ceiling, damn near vertical, before dropping sideways. I flop back and forth, a holiday rag doll. The Christmas lights swirl, and I am alone in the multicolored dark. I shriek and cheer, grinning with joy, and then it happens. My nose crashes into the beast's steel ear.

I'm barfing, crouched on a sticky bathroom floor, regurgitating several gallons of liquor into a jet-black toilet. Also: there are hands on my back, and I don't like to be touched when I'm evacuating my tummy jellies.

"Don't—" I gasp between retches, throwing my elbow backward in a blind strike. "Who's there?"

"Take it easy, Holden."

"Don't touch me." I spin away from the toilet and find myself face-to-face with my father. His red beard has faded to white, his hair is all but extinct, and he's wearing the old hospital scrubs he stole while remodeling the RUSH University Medical Center.

"Half of what you see," he starts, and his voice is sawdusty and faint, like my ears are blowing cobwebs off his vowels. "And none of what you hear."

"It's *fear*, man," I mutter, licking bile from my lips.

My father drops into a crouch. I'm surprised his old knees are so limber. He opens his bullshit mouth, but I cut him off because I've been prepping for our reunion a long time, and the only thing left in my belly is words.

"Let me stop you right there," I say. "Before you get going on whatever lecture you've been saving up all these years, I need you to know I never wanted to quit talking to you, okay? My silence was a matter of survival. Life's miserable enough without living in a constant state of paranoid dread. And that's what you and your lies are: dreadful, bitter, and frightening to normal people like me who want to wake up in the mornings and do our jobs and love who we love. Maybe every Democrat politician really is a fascist. Maybe the Davos dudes really are planning to exterminate the global underclasses. Maybe our food and air and water really are entirely tainted with mind-numbing poison to make us docile, complacent slaves of the modern anarcho-capitalist cyber state. In light of my crippling confusion and agonizing depression, I am tentatively willing to admit that it is entirely possible that all the illegals really *are* smuggling dirty bombs into the sanctuary cities at the behest of a grossly misunderstood Vladimir Putin whose only real goal is to defend humanity against an evil cabal of Jewish-Ukrainian gangsters trying to dominate the world from Hunter Biden's laptop, but please hear me clear when I tell you, once and for always, that I do not give a shit. I *really* and *truly* do not. We are all, all of us, even you, guaranteed to die sad, lost, and alone, but that's okay. In fact, it's better than okay. It's reality. You can't argue with it. You can't vote against it. And you sure as fuck can't shoot it with your bump-stocked AR-15. Your dumbass MAGA revolution might eventually be televised or livestreamed on CloutHub or set to a cute new sound on a blessedly un-Chinese TikTok, but it will *also* be weak and misguided and pointless. Many will die, many more will be born, and most will forget. In the meantime, I want to fuck and laugh and drink myself shitty in peace. If that makes me a sheep, then baaaaah fucking humbug to you. It's not *my* fault you never prepared me to be a good and civilized person. You didn't know how. You never built a steady career or cultivated a healthy marriage or showed me a future worth living. I wanted so badly to become the man you *claimed* to be, the man you *wanted* me to be, but that's just not who I am. And I'm sorry, okay? I'm *really* sorry, and I'm definitely on drugs, but I have to admit, I am genuinely glad to see you. We've got a lot of shit to work through, you and me, but before we tackle all that, you need to stop making *your* problems *my* problems, okay? Stop doing that, and we'll be cool."

"I can't understand a thing you're saying, Holden."

"And my name isn't *Holden*," I say, in the same moment that I realize my father is Fing and Fing is my father. I slam my eyes shut, terrifically embarrassed, but when I open them again, I'm back on the road.

"I'm taking you to the hospital," Fing says, and I shake my head to clear it. Wet pavement ahead shimmers in Fing's high beams, and all I can see through my passenger window is trees and more trees and hook-clawed demons that are hopefully also trees.

"No," I say, gently inspecting my throbbing face with the tips of my fingers. "I don't need a hospital."

"I think you might."

"Medically, yes. But I'm currently uninsured, and I'll be fine with some ice. Would you mind driving me to my mom's place in Hookville?"

"Do you have a car back at Slaton's?"

"I'm on foot."

"You walked fifteen miles through *this* forest?"

"Was that ill-advised?"

"There's some pretty weird dudes who live around here."

"I'm the meanest son of a bitch in the valley," I say, though if my father happens to be one of the weirdos Fing's referencing, then I'm more like second meanest.

"What valley?"

"Would you mind driving me home?"

"If you're *sure* you don't need a doctor . . . then yeah. No prob. Hookville's pretty close."

"Sick, man. I'll owe you. Nice ride, by the way." I run my hand along the supple leather coating the inside of my door. "Is this a Jeep or something?"

"Land Rover."

"Damn, Fing. You fancy."

"I'm honestly not sure how you're conscious right now."

"Practice."

He grimaces, and I get it. I catch my reflection in the side mirror, and I look like somebody face-fucked me with a sledgehammer. My upper lip is split and bloody, and a mangled purple mass has replaced the appendage formerly known as my nose. Bright side: it might be an improvement.

"What's your mom's address?"

I pat my shorts, checking for my phone before remembering I left it in the car with Yivi. "I don't actually know, at present, but I can find her house from the main drag."

"Works for me."

"Sorry to spoil your evening."

"It's no worries."

"Appreciate you," I say, feeling guilty. Shame sloshes around with the booze in my gut. I reach into my pocket and pop another of Yivi's happy pills. It hurts to swallow, but I manage.

"I gotta say, bud . . ." Fing starts, adjusting his grip on the steering wheel. "I know we're not real close friends or whatever, but I'm worried about you."

"Don't be."

"Are you sure everything's okay?"

I sit up straighter in my seat. "Since when is *anything* okay?"

"You want to tell me what's been going on?"

"Not really."

"I respect that." He flips on his turn signal despite ours being the only car on the road. "But I've also gotta put it out there that I think you might be overdoing it with the drinking."

"Thanks for your concern."

"I'm serious."

"As am I, Fing. And while it's been nice to catch up, and I really do appreciate the ride, you can't possibly understand what I'm going through."

"You mentioned your mom's worried you're having a nervous breakdown."

"Did I?"

"You also said you attacked JZ."

"And you're assuming these events have something to do with my alcohol intake?"

"Call me crazy . . . but yeah, bud. Pretty much."

"I've been drinking since I was a child, Fing, and it's never been a problem."

"It seems like you're hurting."

"My face *is* pretty sore."

"And you're going through a breakup?"

"Are you asking because you're interested?"

"I'm in a relationship."

"Too bad. I've always thought you were cute. We'd be good together—as long as you kept your advice to yourself."

Fing nods and returns his focus to the road. I do the same. The highway rambles, and we pass a few shadowy warehouses and billboards for real estate agents with giant teeth. My face is throbbing, but it's a novel sensation. A lot more external than the alternative. "Holy shit," I say, realizing my headache is completely gone.

"What's wrong?" Fing asks.

"Nothing. I'm great."

"Cool, bud. I'm glad you're great. This has been a real fun reunion."

"I'm sorry you had to see me like this."

"I just feel like . . . I dunno . . . like I wanna help you, but you're not letting me."

"I would let you help if I thought your help would help."

"Fair enough."

I offer Fing an apologetic smile as I inspect his clothes, his car, the way he carries himself. I'm no detective, but I get the sense Fing's got money. More money than you can make writing emails for Walmart. That must be why he gets along with his parents. If anyone in my entire cockroach bloodline had earned a decent living before me, I'm sure Thanksgiving would be a much happier holiday. Unfortunately, my mom's parents used to shoot rabbits in their backyard for food, and my father's parents met in a group home. Orphans who grew up to be factory workers. They scraped by until my grandfather died when my father was thirteen. He had a heart attack in bed, and my father, who'd worked as a lifeguard at the local pool, gave him CPR before the paramedics arrived. Grandpa Gunderson was still breathing when they lifted him into the ambulance. When my father tells this story, he always mentions that the EMT told him my grandfather was going to be fine, but he died on the way to the hospital. This lie, intentional or not, is my father's obsession. I think it torments him, and in some respects, it made him who he is. A bitter, distrustful man who fears the world. He used to tell me that he could be dead at any moment, that his inherited heart disease could not be cured or predicted, and that I should watch what I say to him because he might die before I get the chance to tell him I'm sorry.

"I texted Shirley June that I'm with you, by the way," Fing says, out of nowhere, and whatever embarrassment I'd already been feeling metastasizes into a tumor the size of my stomach.

"Why the fuck would you do *that*?" I ask, spitting each word.

"I wanted to know what's been going on with you."

I glare at Fing, furious that he buried this particular lede. Shirley is the account director who worked most closely with Jenny and me, and she was there in Cleveland when shit went sideways. "I already told you most of everything," I say.

"You didn't tell me you only threw a pen at JZ."

"What do you mean *threw* it?" I ask, though unlike Yivi, I am not a particularly stabby person, and I remember it now. We were in a windowless Marriott conference room after I'd convinced the hotel staff to open Jenny's door. I should have left Cleveland the moment I saw her body, but I wasn't thinking straight. I was unwell, vibrating, and JZ said we should still do the pitch meeting in our dead friend's memory. There was a pile of pens in the center of the table, so I grabbed one. Maybe I didn't stab him, but I fucking wish I had.

"And you didn't tell me about Jenny," Fing says softly.

My asshole clenches so hard I almost faint. "That's because it isn't any of your business."

"Fair enough. But I'm very sorry to hear she's gone. I always liked her."

"I doubt she gave three shits about you."

"You're a real fucking jerk, bud—do you know that?"

"I've been informed."

"I don't *need* to be driving you home."

"You also don't *need* to be texting Shirley."

"I can text whoever I want."

"And I can be pissed about whatever the fuck *I* want."

"Why are you so mad I texted her?"

"You invaded my privacy."

"I was trying to figure out how to help you."

"Lemme let you in on a little secret, Fing," I say, shoving my face closer to his. "You see this?" I draw a finger circle around my mangled nose. "This has got fuck all to do with me killing Jenny."

"*You* killed Jenny?"

I flop back into my seat. "I guess Shirley June didn't give you all the deets."

"She told me Jenny took her own life," he says, and when he says it, something odd happens in my newly pain-free skull. It might be another side effect of Yivi's drugs, but Jenny's face appears before me like a specter. She's standing just inside the doorway to her Marriott hotel room, fidgeting with the red Gucci sweatsuit she always wears on work trips, and I'm leaning hard against the doorframe. We're both wasted, but Jenny more than me. I've been running around Cleveland for the past two hours trying to buy her drugs. An awkwardness hangs between us, and I'm wondering if I should head back to my room. Last night, I slept with Jenny in her hotel bed—a relatively normal occurrence given that we often enjoy fucking each other. We tend to do it whenever we get stuck or stressed, and for the past few years, I've been with her more often than Clinton. But we didn't fuck last night. Instead, we kissed a bit, and I held her while she spiraled. JZ is obviously on this trip too. He and Jenny are supposed to be a thing. Unfortunately for her, JZ's got lots of things, including a wife and three kids, and he's spent this entire trip pretending he barely knows her. JZ is undoubtedly an idiot, but he leads all our meetings, equal parts charisma machine and bullshit artist, and right now, Jenny can't take it. I can't much take it either. It's killing us. We both had a long pandemic. The office has reopened, and we're traveling again, but something is missing. Whatever it was that made us a good team and great friends, we've lost it. I think sex might help, but Jenny wants to honor her thing with JZ, and I'm trying to respect that. Part of me doesn't mind the abstinence, but a larger part does. We take turns falling in love. Sometimes it's Jenny. Right now, it's me. I know she's been struggling, but she won't admit it, and I'm too bitter to ask the right questions. Her Gucci sweatsuit hangs loose off her shoulders. Her eyes have caved into her face. She's been drinking even more than usual. Getting nosebleeds. She spent last night wide awake, panicking, saying she couldn't do this anymore, she needed to quit our shitty job, and she didn't want to move to Paris with me. I assumed she didn't mean it. I knew she was hurting, but I thought we could fix it. She just needed some time off, the right drugs, a new perspective. In the meantime, I could help with the drugs. And I did. She's got the bag I bought in her pocket. I told her how sketchy the dealer was, and she told me she didn't care. Now, though, she's got this terrified look in her eyes. I'm asking if she wants me to spend the night again, and she's insisting she's fine. For some reason, I'm believing her. I'm tired, and I'm worried about our presentation, and I need some sleep, and she's closing her door, and I'm lying to myself.

She'll be okay.

She'll be okay.

She'll be okay.

"I bought the drugs she used to do it," I say, as Jenny disappears into her room.

Fing takes a sec to process this before summarizing his thoughts: "Shit."

"Exactly."

"But that doesn't make you a murderer."

"Maybe not."

"Were there any warning signs?"

"Probably." Jenny has disappeared from the eye of my mind, but I can still hear her voice. She used to joke about killing herself a few hundred times a day. We both did. When the going got tough, the humorous suicidal ideation got going. I never thought it was real. We were mutually miserable, but I always figured she was happier than me. She certainly liked our job more than I did, and outside of work, her life was great. She had a swanky apartment that overlooked Lincoln Park. She wore a different pair of Nike high-tops every day. She dined at a different New American restaurant every night. She had memberships to Soho House and Equinox. She could easily afford her various habits. She spoke fondly of college friends I'd never met. She did COVID Zooms with her sisters. Her parents were Evangelical psychos, but she never had to see them. On paper, she had most of what I thought she wanted, and she didn't have any of the chokehold responsibilities that annihilate most normal people. No family, no kids, no mortgage. But it's possible she wanted some of that shit. Sometimes I think she wished I were a different type of person. A real man she could start a real family with. She told me several times that I should break up with Clinton. She said I could move in with her. I don't know why I never did that. Maybe I was scared. Either way, I was devastated when she started sleeping with JZ, and my fucked-up feelings made me a much worse friend. Ruder, shorter, less considerate. I hate not knowing what people are thinking, and I resent when the select few people I love make me work overtime to understand them. We were working hard enough. It was all we did, and it was most of what we talked about near the end. Pointless projects masquerading as a reason to keep living. When I met Jenny, I saw that her career gave her purpose. That's one of the reasons she was such a powerful ally. But maybe she stopped caring as much as I did. Maybe she realized what I've been realizing since she died.

"Hookville," Fing says after a long silence. "Here we are."

I point out the windshield. "The turn's like a half mile up this road."

We pass the quaint red-roofed buildings and the pond-scummy lake. The town looks deserted at night, like a poorly designed Hollywood set for a semimodern Western movie. No country for young queers, and not a single glowing bar or restaurant in sight. A major bummer because I want another drink. I don't *need* one. I just *want* one. Maybe that's progress. But in America, progress is usually temporary.

"Are we getting close, bud?" Fing asks.

"Affirmative." I grunt to clear my throat. "That's my mom's spot right there."

He pulls over and turns on his flashers. "How long are you in town?"

"Just tonight."

"And then what?"

"Who knows." I grab my door handle, but Fing grabs the sleeve of my shirt.

"Wait a sec," he says, tugging me back into my seat. "I'm sorry I went behind your back and texted Shirley."

"Don't worry about it."

"Jenny was an awesome person. And I know she meant a lot to you. I'm not sure if you've still got my number or whatever, but if you ever need to talk or anything, I'm around."

"Thanks." I sit frozen in my seat, unable to move. I avoid Fing's gaze. My parents' house is dark and dead. The Trump flag nailed to the roof ripples in the wind. I can hear Fing breathing. I won't ring Mom's doorbell tonight. I will sleep on the porch instead. This is more of a fact than a decision.

"I kinda want to ask again if you're okay, bud," Fing says. "But you very clearly aren't."

"I'm not. That's true. But for the record, I'm also not crazy."

"I know," Fing says, and for the first time tonight, I'm glad I ran into him. Because I can tell he isn't lying.

EIGHT

I awaken in violence, raging at the bright blue sky, sucking hard to draw breath through my blood-clogged nostrils. The sun is shining. The birds are crying. I'm lying on my parents' porch, and there's an unfriendly shadow looming over me.

"Oh good. He's awake," says a stranger, a large one, pushing the sharp toe of their boot into my swollen cheek.

I twist onto my hip, away from the loathsome boot, and squint into the glare of a sunburst glinting off a windshield. A windshield attached to a relatively nondescript sedan. A sedan that happens to be tan.

"C'mon, bucko. Wake it up. We ain't got all day," the stranger says, jabbing me twice more with their boot.

"Who the fuck are you?" I ask, but it hurts to talk. My nose, my mouth, my cheeks.

"Uh-oh, folks—we've got ourselves a live one."

I roll off the porch and into a mulch bed. Wet strips of splintery birch cling to my palms as I push myself into a crouch. My assailant seems to be a woman-type character. A heavily tanned woman-type character wearing a white fisherman's vest over a black safari shirt. A black Stetson shades her head, and her face is a sun-shriveled lump of leather hiding behind a black N-95. It's an odd ensemble, and the overall effect gives a neo-desperado vibe that matches the silver-plated six-shooter she's got pointed at my face. The Good, the Bad, and the Fugly.

"Easy, bucko," the cowboy woman says. "All I wanna do is chat."

I stare directly into the barrel of her gun, imagining how cool it would be to watch a bullet enter my own eye. "Chat about what?"

"The whereabouts of your runaway travel companion."

"Which companion?" I ask, gesturing around at Mom's decorative shrubs.

"The one who drove a red Toyota Corolla straight smack into a tree last night."

I sit back on my heels as the front door swings open, and Mom emerges from the house toting a pump-action double-barreled shotgun.

"Get that gun out of my son's face," Mom says. "Or I'll blow you right off this porch."

"No need to get feisty, ma'am." The cowboy woman slides her six-shooter into a hip holster. "If you saw this punk do the things I've seen, you'd take similar precautions."

Mom keeps the shotgun trained on her chest. "What is your business here?"

"Yeah, man," I say, taking this opportunity to climb to my feet. "What the fuck is your business here?"

"I'm Taryn Toschi of Toschi Detective Services, and like I already said, all I wanna do is chat." The masked woman doffs her hat, revealing a buzz cut. "Might be nice to do so inside with the AC if y'all are so inclined."

"We can chat right here," Mom says, and I nearly smile.

"Alrighty, ma'am. That's fine. But I'd have an easier time concentrating if you'd kindly point that firearm somewhere else."

"If you can't say what you need to say, right here and right now, then that's just tough turkey," Mom says, ice-cold.

"Tough *turkey*," Toschi repeats, amused. "You are aware, ma'am, that your darling son here is a car thief, a kidnapper, and a fugitive from the law."

"I know about the car." Mom gives me a look that says my days of shotgun-free motherly love may be numbered. "I spoke to his ex-roommate yesterday, and he's not pressing charges."

"And I'm not a kidnapper," I say.

"Well, bucko, I might have to disagree with you there." Toschi's eyebrows knit together into a caterpillar of menace. "You traveled across state lines with a seventeen-year-old runaway by the name of Grace Gravy, and I have it on good authority that her father won't be as quick to drop the charges as your roommate."

"Her *father*?" I ask, wavering on my feet as Toschi uses her cracked Samsung Galaxy to show me a yearbook photo of a lanky girl with an arrowhead chin and a sunshine-yellow ribbon in her dark curly hair. Even without the aggressive black mascara and the wannabe-Harajuku fashion sense, her likeness is unmistakable. And I am somewhere between terrified and furious.

"This is the young lady you left Chicago with, is it not?"

"As far as I know, her name is Yivi."

"Yeeby?"

"*Yivi*. She's my *friend*. We met at an Airbnb."

Toschi gives me a highly disgusted thrice-over. "That's your story?"

"My story's a little longer than that. But a good summary is either Yivi lied to me, or you've got the wrong information."

"My information is stone-cold certifiable, bucko."

"Then I guess Yivi's a liar," I say. "But I can't help you either way because the last time I saw her, she was driving off into a thunderstorm. Now, can you tell me *exactly* what happened?"

"You tell me." Toschi flips through her camera roll and shows me another photo. "This is the wreckage on Highway 2."

My eyes spasm shut. "Jesus fucking Christ, Yivi."

"Her name is *Grace*. And as far as I'm concerned, you're responsible for her disappearance and—quite possibly—her death."

"How could she have disappeared?" Mom asks, looking at the photo over my shoulder. "I thought you said she was driving this stolen car?"

"There's no sign of her at the crash site," Toschi says. "And judging by his face, I'm not fully convinced your son wasn't in the passenger seat when that car went off the road."

"I wasn't," I say, fighting to keep my voice from trembling. "I was at a bar. And if you don't believe me, you can contact Fingerbone Smite."

"Is that a *name*?"

"IT IS IN ARKANSAS!"

"Calm down, Holden," Mom says.

Woozy, I turn away from Toschi's photo and fixate on a strangely familiar rosebush. The bush is planted in the center of Mom's yard, alone in the sea of reddish landscaping pebbles, and despite its inhospitable environment, the roses are somehow in bloom. Fat red blossoms. I didn't notice it yesterday, and it's freaky to see this bush in the wrong yard, the wrong town, the wrong state. It used to live on our front lawn in Franklin Hole.

There are photos of me next to this bush on every childhood birthday. My father planted it shortly before I was born, and Mom used to say the bush and I grew up together. It's a miracle she could even transplant the scraggly bastard. I can't believe we're both still alive.

"Did you hurt this girl, Holden?" Mom asks, yanking me back to the present.

"I'd never hurt anybody but myself."

"We'll let the authorities decide," Toschi says, pulling a pair of handcuffs out of her fishing vest. They dangle in front of my face, swaying like a hypnotist's pendulum.

"Not before we have a look for ourselves," Mom says.

Toschi nods after a moment of contemplation. "Okay with me." She rests a hand on the butt of her six-shooter. "But be warned, if y'all try anything crazy, I will not hesitate. Not for a *second*." Toschi saunters off our porch in the direction of her car. "Believe you me."

I drag ass over to Mom's minivan—the same forest-green Honda Odyssey she's been driving since the late Cretaceous—and flop into the passenger seat. I slam my skull against the headrest, almost wishing my headache would return. Penance for another fuckup. Another lost friend. My worst nightmare perpetrated by the worst person I know: me. A few tears escape my eyes, and I dab my face with my father's shirt.

None of what I fear.

None of what I fear.

None of what I fear.

Mom's door thumps open, and she slithers into the driver's

seat. I can feel her staring, but I refuse to meet her eyes. "Were you aware your friend was a child?" she asks.

I don't even open my mouth to respond. I'm speechless in the sense that I have things to say, but those things exist beyond my desire to speak. *Because c'mon, Mom. It's me.* I may be the ridiculous asshole who flipped out yesterday, but I'm not a freak. I'm not a loser or a pervert. I might not be the man I used to be, but Mom knows that guy, and he could make friends his own age. He could charm whoever needed charming. Even people who used to hate him kind of liked him. Teachers, bosses, rivals. At least I think they did. And Yivi still probably does. Provided she's not . . .

"Holden?"

"No."

"Because when I met her . . . she looked pretty young."

"Guess you need better glasses."

"Holden."

"Will you please stop calling me that."

"I won't stop using your name."

"It's not my name. I changed it."

"You changed the name I gave you?"

"That is correct," I say, briefly tallying all the other things she's given me that I'd also like to change.

"Legally?"

"No."

"Then I'm still calling you Holden."

"Your cooperation is appreciated."

"Give me a fucking break," she spits, and I suppress a smirk. Same old Mom.

"Pretty sure I'm the one who could use a break."

"But I don't understand it." She sighs. "You've got a new

name, a new life, all these secrets, and that poor, beautiful Jenny just took her own life. I don't even know where to start."

"Maybe start with putting the car into reverse," I say, glad to hear Mom was one of the thousands of people who knew Jenny's death was a suicide before I did.

"You know Clinton's claiming you attacked him, right?" Mom asks.

"He's lying."

"Why would he do that?"

"Because accusing others of abuse is the best way to hide actual abuse."

"Maybe that's the case," Mom says. "But he also told me you two had a terrible fight. He said you grabbed him, so he pushed you, and you tripped on something. You fell and hit your head on the coffee table."

"It was a baseball bat," I say as this fun new slice of memory unfogs. "That's what I tripped over."

"A baseball bat?"

"Clinton loves the White Sox."

"Are you trying to be funny?"

"I guess Clinton's not quite lying. But that doesn't mean he's never been abusive. I've been scared to leave him for years, and I knew I couldn't go gently. I was drunk, and I hadn't slept, so I might have gone a little overboard. I think I told Clinton I found him repulsive. I said I hated him, and I hated touching him, and I never wanted to see him again, and after that, things just sort of spiraled."

Mom observes the side of my battered face for a long time, but I continue to avoid her eyes. "Those are very cruel things to say to someone you care about."

"Pretty sure I was quoting you."

"Did you really hit your head?" Mom asks, ignoring my comment.

"On the coffee table," I say, and suddenly, I remember my living room. Not the one I shared with Clinton, but the one in my cracker-box childhood home. Most of our furniture was cheap and ugly, but we had a gorgeous antique coffee table that had belonged to Mom's grandmother. The day that table died, my brother was crying, and my father was angry. He chased Mom across our house. She was provoking him, calling him names, making everything worse. I was only twelve or thirteen, but I had already witnessed my share of shit, and I could tell my father wanted to hurt her this time. He tried to grab her. I got between them. He shoved me aside, and as I fell to the rug, I swung wildly with my fist. The blow found his jaw. I thought for sure he was going to kill me, but instead, he turned. He lifted my great-grandmother's coffee table above his head and smashed it over his knee. In the bitter silence that followed, I felt positive my father loved me. He was violent, crass, and crazy, but he'd killed that table instead of me.

Behind us, Toschi honks. Mom grunts and backs out of the driveway. She follows Toschi's tan Taurus down the quiet street, and I notice that the private detective has a KENNEDY 2024 decal on her rear windshield. More evidence she is deranged.

"I got you some water," Mom says, and I finally meet her gaze. Her shotgun is resting between our seats, and she's holding a green glass bottle of Mountain Valley Spring Water.

I take the water and place my hand on my chest. "God bless you, Mother. God bless you for the water, and double God bless you for believing I'm not a boyfriend-battering, child-stealing pedophile."

Mom frowns, but I can tell she almost wants to laugh. Which

is nice. I used to make her laugh all the time, and I'd like to rekindle that portion of our relationship someday.

"But seriously," I say, "thanks." I pop the cap off the bottle and open my throat. The water tastes amazing. Almost as good as a fifth of chilled Grey Goose on a sunny Soho House afternoon. I chug it and press my temple against the window.

Hang tight, Yiv. I'm on my way.

"I hope your friend's alright," Mom says, rousing me from the not-so-restful nap I've been taking against the door.

I tongue a trickle of nasal blood from my upper lip. "Don't count her out," I say, straightening my spine in the passenger seat. "She's a much better survivor than I am."

"I'd hope so. We haven't even talked about your face. Or why you slept on my porch."

"Good thing I did, or I'd probably be locked in this lady's trunk." I nod at Toschi's Taurus as the road snakes through a ragged glen populated with more dead trees than live ones.

"You could've knocked."

"I didn't want to bother you so late—after everything." I pat the pocket of my shorts to ensure I'm still carrying a few more Q pills. After checking that Mom's not watching, I dry swallow a dose.

"You've still managed to bother me," Mom says, and she might be making a joke.

"I know. And I'm sorry."

"Really? *You?*"

"Yeah," I say, and it's true. "In my defense, you tricked me into coming down here way before I was ready to face your music, so you can't really blame me for going full shithead."

"I don't blame you."

"You don't?"

"I blame myself."

Uh-oh. Guilt-ridden blastoff sequence initiated. "Don't do that," I say.

"I blame myself . . ." Mom repeats, this time with a ridiculously overindulgent sigh. "Because it's my fault that I let you get away from me."

"You're the one who left town."

"I just mean I never should have pushed you to be better than us."

"You think I'm better than you?"

"I think *you* think that. And that's fine. But I never expected you to end up like . . ."

"Like what?"

"Like you *are*."

"Queer?"

"No."

"Drunk?"

"No."

"Mourning the death of my closest friend?"

"No, Holden."

"Then *what*?"

Mom hesitates. "Somewhere along the line, you turned on me."

I try to laugh and end up coughing. An excruciating experience, not dissimilar to practicing fifth-grade math problems while Mom hovered over my second-grade shoulder.

"It's not funny, Holden."

"I know it isn't," I say, dabbing a bit more blood from my nose with the baggy sleeve of my father's shirt.

"We're supposed to be on the same team."

"You mean I'm supposed to believe Joe Biden's a hologram?"

"Holden."

"It really is too bad the liberal Mafia melted my mind with all that gay-porn brainwashing in college."

"Stop."

"Stop *what*?" I say, gradually losing my temper.

"Just stop it."

"Because you don't like it?"

"I can barely believe it."

But you believed me when I was lying, I think but hold my tongue.

"If it's even true," she continues, "then why didn't you ever tell me about it?"

"You know why," I say, recalling the day Mom broke down in front of the TV because Ellen told Oprah she liked girls. It may be an irrefutable fact that my father cut Mom off from her family, but it's also a fact that Mom rarely mentioned her gay sister when I was growing up. I can count on one hand the times I've seen Auntie Lisa in the flesh, and I've never met her so-called roommate.

"Lying is easier," I continue, because there's no sense in escalating this conversation.

Mom takes her eyes off the road to study my messed-up face. "Why do you think that?" she asks.

There are thousands of honest answers to this question, but none of them seems helpful or productive or perfectly true. "What's funny," I start, shifting our argument away from the obvious, "is *you're* the one who turned on me."

"I've never changed who I am or what I believe," Mom says, as if this is (a) something to be proud of, and (b) not a lie.

"Then why'd you stay with Henry?"

"This isn't about him."

"Of course it is," I say, squeezing the empty Mountain Valley water bottle in my lap. "Everything you *say* and *do* and *think* is about him."

"He isn't even here."

"I know."

"He's gone."

"I *know*!" I yell, losing the remainder of my cool. "That's the worst part!"

"There's no reason to raise your voice."

"YES, THERE *IS*! SOMETIMES THERE *IS*! SOMETIMES YOU'VE GOTTA YELL AND SCREAM AND SAY THE LOUD THING LOUDER!"

"I don't understand what you're shouting about."

"Do you really wanna know? Because if you wanna know, I've gotta tell you."

"I don't care," Mom says, defiant as ever. "Say whatever you want. You know I'm not afraid of a fight."

"Obviously," I say, and then I stop. Because she's right. All these years, Mom's always been the first one out of her corner and back into the fray. And now he's gone. He's gone, but she's exactly the same.

"What's wrong?" she asks, suddenly concerned. "What's wrong, Holden?"

"Did you kick him out?" I ask, before I even know why.

"Your father?" Mom's wrinkled neck flesh wriggles as she shakes her head. "He left on his own."

"And you stayed down here for two full years after that," I say, "because you *wanted* to."

"Of course," Mom says, like I'm some sort of moron. "The weather is nicer—and the taxes."

"The *taxes*."

"It's much more affordable."

"You get what you pay for," I say as we pass a field of dull brown horses sniffing one another's asses.

Mom pretends not to have heard my insult, and she doesn't reply for a long while. The Odyssey rumbles over uneven asphalt, following curve after curve as a series of yellow warning signs implore us to slow down or risk losing the road.

"If you didn't make him," I start when I can no longer handle the suspense, "then why did he leave?"

Mom continues to glare out her windshield. "Why are you asking me that?" she says.

"I guess I'm confused."

"Alright. That's fair. But I don't know exactly why he left. I only know he always wanted to. That was the big reason he pushed me to move down here in the first place."

"Seriously?"

"He got involved with this radical group of men online, and they have a big compound somewhere out in the forest around here. I assumed it was just another of his woo-woo pipe dreams. But when I realized he was serious, I didn't try to stop him."

"Why would you?"

"Exactly," Mom says as Toschi's brake lights flash, and our two-car caravan slows below the speed limit. I crank my neck sideways to peek around the sides of the tan Taurus. And then I see it: the smashed-up red hood rising from a knotted green tangle of undergrowth.

"Are you going to look for him?"

"Maybe," I say, searching desperately for signs of Yivi. "First I've gotta find my friend."

"Oh my *God*, Holden." Mom slaps a hand over her mouth,

finally putting eyes on the wreckage. She brakes harder, and we slide to a stop on the shoulder. I pop open my door, and I'm halfway into the roadside weeds when Mom's fingers close around the scabbed-over wounds Yivi left on my forearm.

"Wait," she says.

"What is it?"

"I just need to know: What do you want me to call you besides Holden?"

My jaw flops open. Shock and awe. "Um." I swallow. "I guess I don't quite know yet."

"What do you mean you don't know?"

"I haven't figured it out."

Mom laughs once. "Are you kidding?"

"Don't mock me." I blush, amazed my cheeks are still capable of signaling embarrassment. "I'm working on it."

"Fine." One side of her mouth angles toward a smile, and she releases my arm. "Let me know when you decide."

I tromp through the tall grass, swatting horseflies as they buzz out of the thicket. Mom parked the van a hundred or so feet from the site of the crash, and I'm approaching from the passenger's side. I can't see the full extent of the damage to the driver's seat, but what I can see has already made an impression.

"In case you haven't noticed," Toschi says from the roadside hill, "it looks a lot worse in person."

"Where are the police?" Mom asks.

"Guess nobody rang them . . ."

"You didn't tell them a little girl's *missing*?"

"I'm a small-business owner, ma'am. If my employer instructs me to leave the authorities out of a case, I don't bite the hand that pays."

I clench my aching teeth, unsure whether I'm pissed the cops weren't notified or grateful that no one is here to arrest me. "When you say *employer*, you mean Yivi's father?" I ask.

"*Grace's* father." Toschi tromps down from her perch, following me through the tall grass. "Doctor George Gravy. He's a very successful psychiatrist."

I almost chuckle, but I'm short on mirth. Besides, I've reached the car. I hold my breath, picking careful steps as I work my way around the trunk. I know Yivi isn't here, but I'm terrified of what I might find in the driver's seat. I swallow a thick cord of snot and clear my throat, preparing myself. Then, I jump, startled by a thumping sound.

"Yivi?" I wheel around, triangulating noises until I locate the source of the thump: the backseat. I lunge sideways and tear open the rear door, but there's nothing except shattered glass and a perfectly unshattered bottle of Bacardi. Confused, I grab the rum I borrowed from Mom's house and listen harder. A low and resonant banging.

"Is anybody else hearing that?" I ask, hoping my head injury hasn't evolved into full-blown schizophrenia.

"Hearing *what*, bucko?"

I strain my ears. I jog around the big tree, recheck the backseat, and search the undercarriage of the car. But . . . nothing. I massage the muscles in my jaw.

"What's wrong, Holden?" Mom asks, picking her way down the damp easement.

"That thumping sound," I say, inspecting the driver's seat to find the limp carcass of an airbag and a relatively intact cockpit.

Even my iPhone in the center console is completely unbroken. Wherever Yivi is, she's probably alive.

"You better not try anything funny," Toschi says.

"Shut up for a sec." I fumble with my phone, but it's dead.

"Don't te—"

"Shu—"

"Don—"

"STOP!" A muffled shout slices through our argument.

"Yiv? Hey, *Yiv*? Is that you?"

"STOP!"

"You'd better watch the way you talk to me, bucko," Toschi says as I realize the shouting is coming from the trunk.

"STOP!"

"YIVI?!" I stumble back to the driver's seat, lightheaded and thrilled. I feel along the floor for the switch that opens the trunk, popping both the hood and the gas cap before I locate the correct release.

"STOP!" Yivi shouts again as the trunk springs open.

"It's *her*!" Mom says.

"I'll be dazzled and damned," Toschi says, beating me to the trunk. When I arrive, Yivi's asleep, tossing punches at what looks like a moldy gym bag. A rip down the center of her Panama Jack T-shirt exposes her belly, and bruises raccoon the edges of her eyes, but otherwise, she seems okay.

"Wake up, dummy," I say, grabbing Yivi's shoulder and shaking her awake. Her body spasms, and her eyes flicker. I dodge her Nosferatu fingernails as she makes a play for my arm. Mom says something behind me, but I keep all five senses locked on Yivi as she works her mouth into a scowl as jagged as her claws.

"What the fuck do *you* want?" she asks, and I grin, trying my damnedest not to weep because seeing my favorite liar, safe and sound and seething, it feels good—the same way I used to feel with Jenny sometimes, in those rare moments when the sky shimmered and gravity ebbed, and I knew things might be okay, if only for a little while longer.

NINE

Yivi flails, struggling to tame her gangly teenaged limbs. With visible effort, she worms her way into a seated position, managing to give me the stink throughout the entire maneuver. Clearly, she has not forgiven my various trespasses.

"Hey, Yiv," I say. "Missed you."

"Who the fuck are *you*?" Yivi asks, aiming her fury at Toschi.

Toschi has raised her phone above the trunk, evidently capturing video. "Hello there, Grace. I'm Taryn Toschi of Toschi Detective Services. Please don't be alarmed. You're safe now, and your father says hello."

Yivi's mouth implodes into a devastated O, and her body shrinks to seventeen-year-old proportions.

"Yi—" I start.

"YOU BROUGHT THEM HERE?!" she shrieks.

"Under duress."

"Has this unstable alcoholic man been hurting you?" Toschi asks as she unholsters her gun.

"WHAT THE HELL IS HAPPENING?!"

"Pretty sure this lady's the cowboy from your dreams."

"What'd I say about pulling that gun around my kid?" Mom says, and I smile because she didn't say *son*.

"WHY DOES EVERYBODY HAVE GUNS?!"

"I'm just trying to make sure you're safe," Toschi says. "Now, please, ma'am, lower your weapon."

I swivel my head a fraction, and Mom has resumed brandishing her shotgun. It's possible she doesn't understand the concept of escalation, but if the worst thing that happens today is Yivi gets soaked in my briny brain matter, that's probably a win for all involved.

"Let's not push it, Mom," I say. "This chick almost shot me yesterday morning."

"*Yesterday?*" Mom asks.

"Wait, wait, wait." Yivi clambers to her feet in the bed of the trunk. "Everybody needs to chill the fuck out right now."

"Chilling out's going to be a tad bit tough, Yiv, because your dad's private detective wants to throw me in jail for supposedly kidnapping you due to the as-yet-unverified fact that you're a seventeen-year-old kid whose real name is Grace Gravy."

"Wait—*what*?" Yivi asks.

"I know, right? Pretty wild."

"Nobody *kidnapped* me."

"Told you," I say, mostly to my mom.

"And screw my stupid dad for sending this fake fucking rent-a-cop to babysit me like I'm not a grown-ass woman."

Toschi's shoulders sag. "Seventeen is hardly, as you say, *grown-ass*."

"I'm *eighteen*," Yivi says. "My stupid birthday was last week."

"Oh, damn," I say. "Happy birthday." I toast her with the Bacardi bottle and take a much-needed sip.

"Happy birthday," Mom and Toschi repeat, simultaneously.

"But birthdays aside," Toschi continues, "your father wants you home safe and . . ." She appraises Yivi's bloody T-shirt. ". . . mostly sound."

"But I hate my dad," Yivi says.

"Relatable," I say.

"Be that as it may," Toschi starts, heaving a breath that portends a soliloquy of standards and responsibilities. Before she can unleash her diatribe, however, Yivi leaps, gazelle-style, out of the trunk and into a lime-green patch of elephant ear weeds.

"Fuck this," she says, stumbling over a mossy log before taking off—at a rather unimpressive top speed—into the woods.

Toschi scowls at Yivi's bouncing back. "Fuck this *indeed*." She holsters her gun.

"You'd better go after her," Mom says to me. "She could hurt herself out there all alone."

I shove my tongue behind my swollen upper lip. It goes without saying that I'm in no physical shape to pursue a high school student through the forest at high noon on a 150-degree day, but I suppose most of this is my fault. "Cool with you if I give chase?" I ask Toschi.

"I've already got enough chigger bites for one lifetime." She lifts the brim of her Stetson and gives me a hard appraising look. "And you're not even so bad," she says.

"Thanks, I guess."

"Be careful out there, Hol—" Mom stops herself. "Hon."

For someone so lanky and lean, Yivi doesn't move too quick. Clearly not a secret high school track star. She'd better work on her fast-twitch muscle fibers if she expects to continue this juvenile-runaway thing with any success.

"Where do you think we're even going, Yiv?"

"Stop fucking chasing me."

"I'd prefer to think we're racing each other to death." I hold my pace a few lengths behind her, maintaining a nonthreatening distance. This isn't the kind of forest with footpaths, and the going is rough and rude. Stumpy yellow weeds and sad brown bushes slice my bare calves. And this heat. I desperately require hydration, but the only liquid at hand is this quarter-full bottle of Bacardi I'm using like an IV drip.

"I hate you so much, I can't even stand it," Yivi says, hopping over a yellowish creek and nearly losing her footing. Her fannypack is slung over her shoulder, bouncing wildly against her hip. I consider grabbing the strap to impede her progress, but that feels unfair.

"But what if I'm sorry?"

"Fuck off."

"You're the one who lied about your entire identity."

"FUCK *OFF*!"

"You already said that." I set my teeth and suck wind through a grimace. "And believe me, I'd *really* like to, but I can't in good conscience leave you alone out here."

Yivi says nothing and accelerates up a hillside, gassed and furious and desperate to prove she can make it on her own. I get that. I was eighteen once, and I don't feel much older now.

"Will you at least tell me why you're running from your dad?" I ask, once I've gathered enough damp oxygen to continue our conversation.

"Same reason you stopped talking to yours."

"That's pretty improbable."

"You said you hate him and everything he stands for."

"I'm not sure that's a direct quote, but I do believe I was pretty drunk when I intimated something to that effect."

"Then I guess you lied."

"You know I didn't."

"I don't know shit."

I glare at the sweat-and-blood-soaked Panama Jack T-shirt clinging to her bony hips. "Are you really gonna make me chase you all the way across Arkansas?" I ask. "Or are you gonna act like the adult you've been pretending to be and tell me why you've been making up stories for the entirety of our friendship?"

"Fuck off," Yivi says, but this time, she glances at me over her shoulder. We lock eyes for the first time since I let her drive Dante's Corolla into a thunderstorm. Then she trips over a rock.

"Holy shit—are you okay?" I drop into a crouch.

"Why can't everyone just leave me alone?" Yivi says between sobs. She's writhing on her side, grasping her shin. What's left of yesterday's mascara pours through the channels of her cheeks, borne by sweat and fury and tears.

"Maybe because you're the best and everyone likes you?"

Her eyes flash, hotter than the high noon sun. We aren't in a clearing, but the surrounding trees aren't providing much canopy. The dirt underfoot is damp but hard, and something—either a rodent corpse or my armpits—is lending the odor of rotting flesh to our midday melodrama. "You don't even know what you're talking about," Yivi spits.

"I would if you'd tell me," I say, hefting the Bacardi once more to my lips.

She mocks me with a snort. "Fucking alcoholics."

"I'm working on that."

"*Sure* you are." She releases her shin. It looks fine, not even skinned. "And so's my dad."

"He's a drinker?"

"I really don't wanna talk about this shit."

"That's super fair—but at some point, I'd really appreciate an explanation."

"You know, babe, for someone who says they're not a man anymore, you sure fucking act like one most of the time."

I take another sip of yesterday's rum and adjust the stance of my crouch. "I don't know what to say to that."

"Maybe don't say *anything*," she says, clenching her fingers around invisible balls of rage. "Maybe that's the point. Maybe just shut the fuck up and leave me alone. Cuz I was fine before I met you. I was *fine*, and I was *free*, and I was actually having a lotta fun figuring out what I was gonna do with the rest of my life. But then *you* showed up, and you tricked me into thinking we were friends, and now I'm gonna get shipped back to Indiana."

"Indiana?"

"Is that seriously the only thing you heard?"

"I'm just surprised a cool chick like you came out of Mike Pence's rat pasture."

She laughs her way into a growl that gradually becomes the words "Shut up."

"I'm only trying to lighten the mood."

"But that's exactly why I can't tell you stuff: You *never* take me seriously."

"Maybe not on the outside."

"But the outside's all I see, babe." Yivi drops her gaze to the ground. "I wanted to tell you so bad so many times, but I knew you'd make jokes and talk down to me even more than you already do."

"Well, fuck me," I mutter, looking around. This clearing seems to be at the top of a short prominence. We're at most a fifteen-minute walk back to the road, but the forest feels endless. "I know I'm an asshole sometimes, Yivi," I continue, "but I'd never intentionally talk down to you. If anything, I think you're more mature than me."

"Don't gimme that bullshit." She wipes her cheeks with a handful of T-shirt collar. "I'm really not in the mood."

"I told you: honesty only."

"Do you have any idea how stupid that sounds?"

"I'm vaguely aware."

"I'm trying to have a *real* conversation about the *real* world, and you're living some fantasy where you're Pinocchio learning life lessons, and all the rest of us are mean old dwarves."

"I'm not Pinocchio."

"Then talk to me like a person."

"What exactly do you want me to say, Yiv? I literally chased you all the way out here because I was worried, and I'm not even mad that you pretended you were being stalked by a drug dealer ex-boyfriend who turned out to be your dad."

"If you're really not mad, then be nice to me."

I thumb a tight ball of fascia at the base of my neck. "I *am* being nice," I say, battling the urge to take another sip of rum. "And I'm serious about being honest. There are real life-and-death consequences to this shit."

"I'm the one who almost died."

"Don't remind me."

"And you can't blame me for lying."

"I'm not," I say as a large reddish bird floats past and alights on a branch. The bird gives me a long judgmental look, then commences ripping the head off a rodent. I watch it dine for a while, chewing and tearing the flesh. It's a nasty business, but life goes on.

"These past few weeks haven't really seemed real to me," Yivi says.

"I don't disagree."

A pale lump of rock lies half-buried in the mud between Yivi's legs. She wraps her hand around one end, trying to wriggle it free. "I keep wondering: *How'd I even get here?*"

"Todd's plan, I guess."

"I dunno, babe," she says. "I think the thing I hate most about being alive is it's ridiculously easy to imagine your life good, but it's almost impossible to make the good things actually happen."

"That might be true for other people, Yivi, but I'm pretty sure *you* could do it—even if you'd rather spend your time drinking with losers and cosplaying poverty."

A nasty swarm of gnats orbits Yivi's head as she digs twin troughs along the sides of the rock, determined to continue her excavation. Her nails are cracked and grimy, and with her hair slicked back against her scalp, she's starting to resemble Smeagol. "You're not *actually* a loser," she says.

"Thank you for saying so."

"And I'm not cosplaying poverty."

"You're not?"

Yivi shoves her fingers beneath the rock, twisting until it slowly emerges from the ground, much longer and odder than expected. "You might not understand what I'm going through, but that doesn't mean you get to make fun of it," she says.

"You're right," I say. "I'm sorry."

"Look how weird this thing is." She smacks a couple dirt clods from the ends of her archaeological discovery. "I've never seen a rock like this before," she continues, and then it hits me.

"Whoa, Yiv, wait—"

She lifts the terrible object higher with both hands. It's caked with grime and soil, but the shape is unmistakable: a recently buried bone that looks way more human than animal.

"OH *NO*!" Yivi flinches, her hands spasming as she tosses the bone through the air. It bounces a few times before settling like death into the dirt. Suddenly, the forest seems alive with movement and monsters.

Yivi scrabbles to her feet. "I really don't wanna be out here anymore, babe."

"Same," I say, lurching back toward the road. "Let's bounce."

"Funky," Yivi says, stopping at the foot of a massive fallen tree, cleaved down the middle by a lightning strike. The twin halves of the blackened tree trunk stretch off in opposite directions, forming a literal fork in the road. "Which way?" she asks.

"What if my answer is *neither*?"

"Then I think we should just quit here and die."

"Your optimism is inspiring," I say, though I see her point. We've been walking for what feels like hours, and I'm pretty positive we picked the wrong direction.

Yivi sweeps some sweaty curls off her face. She takes an exploratory step to the left, then the right, then pauses. The underbrush gets thicker in both directions, and her bare knees are starting to remind me of Pinhead's haircut. "I'm crazy thirsty," she says.

"How about this way?" I point, struggling to lift my arm. "Nature's slightly thinner, so it'll be easier walking, and if it feels wrong after a bit, we can always turn back."

Without a word, Yivi agrees. We trudge along for several exhausting minutes. I try not to focus on my sore feet or my chafed crotch or my nasal bones that are probably already healing wrong, but ignoring those things causes my mind to conjure imagery of cannibals munching femurs like Popeyes drumsticks. The worst part: All the cannibals look like Dante.

None of what I fear.

None of what I fear.

None of what I fear.

"Tell me something fun," Yivi says.

"Have you ever heard of the valley of the shadow of death?" I ask, eyeing the last few rum drops dancing in the bottom of my bottle.

"It doesn't sound very fucking fun."

"No." I tug the vestigial hairs sprouting from my chin. "But relevant." For Yivi's sake, I rack my pathetic memory for amusing anecdotes. "Oh wait," I start, "I did have this weird thing happen to me last night, and I guess I could classify it under *fun*."

"Tell me."

"This is pretty random," I say as I high-step my way through the undergrowth. "But basically, I ended up at this weird Christmas bar after me and you parted ways, and I ran into this guy who used to be my intern."

"So what?"

"So . . . I knew him in *Chicago* . . . but he lives *here* now."

"Weird coincidence." Yivi kicks a rock that I'm pretty sure isn't a human bone. "Did you guys get wasted and smash in the bathroom or something?"

"He's in a relationship."

"This isn't a very fun story."

"I guess not." I pause to scrape a sharp knot of dried blood from the inside of my nostril. "But while we were catching up, he told me Jenny killed herself."

"That doesn't surprise me," Yivi says, and I'm shocked by the immediacy of her candor.

"But I told you—"

"She took your sketchy murder pills in a hotel room, babe. That's basically a classic suicide scenario. Plus, nobody spikes Xanax with fentanyl."

I frown at my nearly eradicated sneakers. "These are good points," I say.

"For the record, if I'd ever even *kinda* believed you were actually a murderer, I woulda bailed way back in Missouri."

"For your sake, I hope that's true."

"It's truer than true, babe. You might think you're scary, but I've known you were a mostly good person since the moment I met you. I'm psychic, remember?"

"Another of your unforgivable deceptions."

"It's not *my* fault you're so gullible."

"And it's not *my* fault you're a fraud."

"Sorry," Yivi says with a giggle. "Though, in my defense, I wasn't, like, fully lying about the dream stuff."

"What do you mean?"

"Cops . . . Cowboys . . . Forest priests . . ." Yivi tosses me a seemingly earnest shrug. "My nightmares are a vibe."

I stumble around the perimeter of a wide boulder, trying to decide whether I'm willing to believe her this time, and a strange sound catches my attention. Like someone—or some*thing*—stepped on a stick. "Did you hear that?" I ask.

"Hear *what*?"

"That sound."

"Sure hope it's not a FOREST PRIEST!"

"Shut up."

Yivi doubles over laughing.

I resist the urge to kick her. "I know you think you're hilarious," I say. "But my mom *literally* just told me that my father might be living out here in these woods because he apparently joined some type of old-guy cult, so excuse me if my sense of humor's kind of busted."

"Wait," Yivi says, still laughing. "Are you being serious?"

"Yes."

Yivi pauses to scrutinize me with a new and humorless look. "Is that why we're still out here?" she asks.

"What?" I blink. "No."

Her mouth twitches into a smirk. "Did you, like, get us lost on purpose just so you could look for him?"

"That's not even funny."

"Are you sure?"

"I don't even know if I want to find him," I say, and we both lapse into silence. We trudge the length of a deep damp gulch, the muddy ground slopping beneath our soggy soles—a remarkably similar walking experience to the summertime nature hikes my father and I took through the mountains of Idaho. Scotchman Peak. Table Rock. Fishhook Creek. A civilized life has never held much appeal for Henry Gunderson, and he spent those hikes laughing and yodeling, hopping from rock to rock, leading us onto forbidden cliffs while I lagged behind, begging him to stick to the trail. I might not have realized it at the time, but I think my father had hoped that trip would bring us closer together. As such, I'm sure he was fairly upset when I demanded we head home early. It was a very important emergency—boyfriend problems with Clinton—but I couldn't exactly tell my father that. Instead, I told him I thought the trip was crazy and pointless. We didn't talk much on the car ride home, and we never did find a place to bury his fallout shelter.

Yivi clears her throat like she's gargling gravel. "And how does that make you feel?" she asks, apparently reading my thoughts.

"I'm not quite sure, Doctor Gravy, but I appreciate the psychoanalysis."

"Fuck off."

"You know, if someone were to calculate your attitude toward me using the frequency and intensity with which you tell me to *fuck off*, they might conclude you're a lot less angry now than you were a few hours ago."

"Whatever helps you sleep at night."

"And speaking of *earlier*," I say as the terrain shifts, and we begin hiking uphill. "Do you mind explaining how you got yourself stuck in that trunk?"

Yivi waves her hand, swatting a gumball-sized horsefly as she dismisses my inquiry. "I wasn't *stuck*," she says. "I was *hiding* in case someone creepy saw the car from the road and decided to proactively punish me for all the abortions I'm destined to have." She shoots me a melodramatic look, and we both burst out laughing.

"Can't say I blame you," I mutter, rubbing my last few drops of bodily moisture from my eyes.

"What's even funnier is I'm basically serious," Yivi says. "It was pouring, and the car was pretty stuck after I bumped into that tree. I figured I should get some shut-eye and wait for morning before I hoofed it back to town, but I didn't feel safe in the backseat where someone could see me. Plus, the trunk was kinda comfy."

"Your narcoleptic abilities never cease to impress."

"It's my only legit skill in life."

"False," I say, and Yivi stops walking.

"Whoa, whoa, whoa, babe," she says. "Wait a sec."

I stop too and scan the forest. I'm about to ask what her problem is when I see it: an odd wooden cave that looks man-made.

"Holy shit, there's more of them," she says . . . and she's right. All around us, cave-like dwellings crouch like creepy humps of nightmare. Wood-thatched teepees with curved roofs. Old and dark and extremely uninviting.

"Summer homes for boogeymen," I say, stepping backward into some weedy brush. "Let's get the fuck outta here." I turn, but more hovels loom in the woods up ahead. Heavily weathered. An M. Night Shyamalan village hidden in plainish sight by the summertime overgrowth, as if it was abandoned a few years back.

"Do you think Native Americans built them?" Yivi asks.

"Native Americans generally shop at Home Depot," I say, and the forest erupts with extremely odd giggles. "Did you hear that?" I ask. "Or am I tripping off these drugs?"

"I heard it." Yivi shivers my timbers with a hard-eyed look. "And you didn't tell me you were on drugs."

"It's only the Q."

"Y'all nice folks shouldn't be doing no drugs," the Giggler says, and I flinch.

"Who's out there?" Yivi asks.

The Giggler giggles again. "More like *in* here," they say.

"We should run," I say as Yivi strides like a fool toward the nearest hovel.

"It's coming from that one," she says.

"What're you doing?"

"I'm gonna ask for directions."

"But they sound nuts."

"Don't be ableist." Yivi is halfway to the structure, and I follow her because if she gets gutted from head to toe by a hook-handed hillbilly maniac, I'll feel at least mostly responsible.

"Happy birthday, babies," the Giggler says as we draw nearer.

"Excuse me?" Yivi asks, ridiculously polite. "Do you know the way to the nearest town?"

"Happy birthday to me," the Giggler sings, softly, almost sweetly. "Happy birthday to you, happy birthday to me, happy birthday America, happy birthday, you're doomed."

"Goddamnit, Yivi," I whisper. "Let's go before you get us both killed."

"Somebody better blow my candle," the Giggler says, and a pinkish creature hops out from behind the nearest, thickest tree. A white guy, tall and fat and nude, lands with a branch-breaking thud in front of the hovel.

"We should go," Yivi says, throwing her feet in reverse.

"I'M A MANLY MAN, SEXY BABIES!" the Giggler screams, gyrating his pubis in a loose circle. "AND GOD DONE MADE ME SO PRETTY!"

"Run, Yivi!" I shout as the Giggler dances toward her.

"I fucking hate Arkansas," she says, darting past me as I turn to follow.

"You're not gonna wanna head that way, my babies!" the Giggler shouts.

"Why not?" Yivi shouts back.

"Don't run from paradise!"

"Stop listening to him," I say, gasping.

"PAST THIS HERE POINT, ALL YE SHALL PERISH!"

I sprint a few awkward paces, hopping over a series of saplings. I can hear the Giggler crashing through the underbrush behind us, and I'm neck and neck with Yivi when I step on an unnervingly soft and squishy mass. My shoe slips sideways, and I hit the ground, palms sliding through grit and grime and worms.

"Gross, gross, gross," Yivi says, grabbing my hand.

I peek down at my Balenciagas, and they're smeared with sticky blood. I shriek, worried I've mangled my feet, but the soft thing I tripped over seems to be a festering deer carcass infested with hundreds of beetles. I cover my face as the scent becomes everything, and the force of my hand slapping my nose hurts so badly, I almost lose consciousness. But I don't. Instead, I'm wide awake when something incredibly heavy drops from the branches overhead and pins me and Yivi to the ground.

"I'm a real man," the Giggler says for what must be the fiftieth time in the last few minutes. He's kneeling near my face, smiling at me through a rope net. His teeth are brown nubs, his beard a wild knot, and I can't tell who stinks worse: me or him or the deer.

"Do something, babe," Yivi whimpers. "I'm really scared." I can feel her writhing, but I can't turn my head. Her fingers twitch against mine. I grab her hand and squeeze.

"I won't let him hurt you," I say, screwing my eyes shut as my dumbass lizard brain struggles to devise an escape plan. I have obviously never been trapped beneath a net before, but I'm surprised it's this uncomfortable. The weight is murder on my lower back, and the rocks digging into my cheek are most definitely damaging my complexion. Also, there are beetles trying to crawl inside my throbbing nose.

"What you done seen and what you done heard," the Giggler says, "that ain't never what's done happened."

"I'll give you money if that's what you want," I say, though

I have a feeling this naked dude isn't interested in my material possessions. He is clearly mentally ill, and I am fairly certain Yivi and I are about to die. With that in mind, I am frankly disappointed. I've always hoped that, near the end, my whole life would flash before my eyes. Head injuries aside, my memory rarely works like it should. Most people seem capable of recalling insignificant or even pleasant events—like the first time they saw *Rush Hour 2* or exactly where they were the day Bin Laden got shot in the face—but I can't remember anything of the sort. Even under the cheerful influence of Yivi's happy pills, my memories come to me in flashes and fragments, usually the most unpleasant moments, and only in the form of low-res, black-and-white VHS video clips. Unlike my father, I do not believe in an afterlife, but I still wonder whether, upon dying, I will be judged. I wonder what questions the immovable mover will ask of me. If pressed, I don't think I could explain who I was or why I acted the way I did. I lack the necessary data, and even if the entirety of my memory reappeared with Technicolor clarity, I doubt I could draw any reasonably authentic conclusions. For me, the past is its own conspiracy theory. If I could remove one pivotal experience from my mind and present it to the entire internet as some vague approximation of my own Zapruder film, I am sure the discourse would be toxic, confusing, and idiotic. There are a handful of events that occur to me as I conduct this thought experiment—masturbating to David Bowie when I had my first orgasm, fleeing my first college party because a bro called me a faggot, asking Clinton to be my sponsor at my first and last Alcoholics Anonymous meeting—but the one that occurs to me most strongly is also the subtlest. At some point during the pandemic, a long time after my Chili's confessional, Jenny and I were naked in her apartment. She was standing before her big bedroom window, gazing down at the white and wintry expanse of Lincoln Park. I was sitting on the tousled bed behind her. The light was soft the way light usually gets when you briefly forget you're fucked, and I was preparing to tell Jenny that I wanted to leave Clinton. Before I could do so, though, she asked me, ostensibly out of nowhere, why I *wanted* to identify as genderqueer. She said I *looked* like a man, and I *sounded* like a man, and I *fucked* like a man, so why not just *choose* to be *that*? To be absolutely clear, Jenny was a liberal. She believed in liberty and equality. She hated her MAGA Evangelical parents, she marched for George Floyd, and she frequently referred to J. K. Rowling as a *TERF-ass bitch*. I felt safe when I was with her, and I had even convinced her to stop calling me *Daddy* during sex. To say that, at the time, I was speechless, is a massive understatement. Even now, as I writhe in the buggy muck of this torn-up deer carcass, I am still speechless. If pressed or tortured or commanded at gunpoint by Saint Peter's Heavenly Gestapo, I don't think I could convincingly defend the legitimacy of my gender. Sexuality is easy. Regardless of genitals, most attractive people give me erections. This is eminently provable. But I don't know how to convince anyone that I've never, never in my life, felt like a man or a woman. I couldn't fully convince the person who mattered most to me, and when I die, if I do happen to see Jenny in some unlikely existential epilogue, I doubt I'll even bring it up.

The Giggler leans closer to my face, and I can smell the hepatitis on his breath. "Y'all kiddos are in for a world of wonders." He pokes a black-stained finger through the net and, with a quick and surprisingly tender flick of his wrist, taps the tip of my nose. "Boop," he says.

"Get your nasty hobo hands off me," I say, attempting to

sound menacing while I mentally transmit a prayer to Vissarion, Gaia, Sugmad, and all the rest of Henry Gunderson's Pantheon, asking them to send my father like a mighty razorback to throttle this creepy maniac.

The Giggler wiggles a loose canine tooth with his tongue. "How 'bout Brucey gives your lady a little boop, then?" He stands and limps out of view.

"Babe?" Yivi whispers, and her voice is really rattling.

"Hidey-ho, my pretty baby."

"DON'T YOU FUCKING TOUCH HER, YOU REDNECK PIECE OF SHIT!"

"What have you got there, Bruce?" asks someone whose voice is a lot deeper than the Giggler's.

"Oh no," Yivi says.

"What's happening?" I ask as a freshly foreboding set of footsteps snaps, crackles, and pops through the underbrush.

"It's forest priests, babe. *Forest* priests."

"Lookee now, boys." The Giggler squeals with perfect delight. "Look what old Brucey done caught here in paradise."

Two more middle-aged white men, both wearing white robes and white moccasins, step into view from my left. Instead of approaching, they circle us, strolling in a wide, leisurely arc. I consider calling out to them, and I wonder how well they know the Giggler. As nervous as their presence is making me, I'm glad they're wearing clothes. Their outfits aren't exactly normal, but after spending most of yesterday in a bloodstained Motel 6 bathrobe, it feels wrong to judge.

"What's happening, babe?" Yivi whispers.

"They're talking."

"About what?"

"Good question." I twist my head for a better look, but the robe-clad men have moved into my blind spot. I can hear them arguing in hushed tones, probably about which of them gets to eat my big, tasty ass. "Can somebody please get this fucking net off our backs?" I say, when I can no longer contain my desire to run my mouth.

"Why didn't you just say so before?" the Giggler says, and a fraction of a second later, we're miraculously freed.

I roll over to find our naked friend holding a rope connected to the net via some kind of tree-branch pulley. He flashes his nubby brown teeth as Yivi springs to her feet, ready for battle. I wipe roughly two thousand beetles off my shirt and heave myself into a vaguely upright position. A head rush tosses a buzzing veil over my face, and I stumble sideways, stepping directly into the belly slime of the mangled deer. The squishing sound is deeply upsetting, and the soggy gore rushes up and floods the tattered remains of my seven-hundred-dollar sneaker.

"Y'all folks are trespassing," says one of the robe-clad men, and I spin toward his voice. He's sporting a long, braided beard. His biceps rival the size of my head, and he's holding a spear that would frighten most grizzly bears. I do not know what to make of his appearance, but my best guess is that Yivi and I have stumbled upon a strange Arkansas cult that has combined CrossFit with traditional Native American reenactment.

"You must be a long way from home," says the second robe-clad man as he inspects the sorry state of our clothes. His beaded necklace is more impressive than Braidbeard's, and a series of white feathers are woven into his gorgeous brown hair. Perhaps this backwoods CrossFit cult makes its own natural shampoo.

"We weren't aware this was private property," I say, doing

my best to sound contrite while I casually prep for combat. My shoulders tense, my knees flex, and my balls retract. Unfortunately for Yivi, I'm not much of a brawler. The only fight I've ever actually won was against my father. After the coffee table incident—which I don't really consider a fight—he became less overtly violent with our family. He shoved Mom a few times, and she sprained her ankle pretty badly during one of their squabbles, but aside from the constant verbal abuse, he mostly calmed down. Maybe my twelve-year-old fist had knocked something loose in his skull. Or maybe his frequent unemployment and increasingly noticeable depression made him more docile. Either way, we trod carefully around one another while I was in high school, and things improved a bit after I left for college. Moving out of my parents' place was good for our relationship, and while the road trip out west was a bust, it still proved my father and I could spend something approximating quality time together. When I started working, my parents didn't like asking me for money, but they appreciated that I was willing to help them. We got along like America and post-Soviet Russia, me growing stronger while they were too weak to make any trouble. But Trump changed all that. His campaign lit a fuse, and Thanksgiving 2016 blew my family apart. I hadn't seen my family since the election, and while this was before my brother met his wife, he didn't come home from London. I don't blame him. Thanksgiving has always been a depressing and isolating day in our house. No relatives to warm our table. Just cheap ham, canned cranberry sauce, and too much time to speak our minds. Mom had specifically requested that we avoid talking politics during dinner, but we got there anyway when my father asked me why I hadn't invited Jenny to Thanksgiving. He told me he could tell she was a real woman, a real housewife like Mom, and not the kind of uppity liberal bitch who wanted a limp-wristed city boy. This was obviously absurd, given that my father literally grew up in the city of Chicago and Mom was never actually a stay-at-home wife, but my sense of humor failed me. I can't remember exactly what happened to force the moment to its crisis. I do remember, however, that I was extremely drunk. In an unreasonable rage, I knocked my father out of his chair, wrestled him to the floor, and punched him three or four times in the face before I noticed he wasn't fighting back. I was crying. So was Mom. She was trying to pull me off his body, saying I was going to kill him, a typical exaggeration on her part, but I did break his flat pig nose. Blood on my hands, blood in his beard, and that was the end. In hindsight, it was largely my fault. I shouldn't have gone home for dinner. I shouldn't have killed a fifth of Smirnoff on the Metra. And I shouldn't have expected my father to act like anyone other than himself.

"Let's eat!" the Giggler shouts. "Who wants a kiss?"

"Please forgive our very confused friend," Featherhair says, his tone somber and, to my happy surprise, apologetic.

"I'll forgive him if he stays away from her," I say, gesturing to Yivi.

"I'll fucking kill him if he tries anything," she says, and this time, I am much less shocked to see she's brandishing her knife. Her insistence on threatening to stab everyone we meet is somewhere between endearing and incredibly annoying, but at present, I don't blame her. Braidbeard's got that spear—which upon further examination seems to be a rusty kitchen knife strapped to the end of a long wooden staff—and Featherhair's got a bigger blade than Yivi's hanging from his belt. Both men are taller than us, and both look as if they've killed before.

"I assure you, he won't be trying anything," says Featherhair as he and his robe-clad partner step closer. "Bruce used to be a member of our tribe, but his instability made it difficult for us to accommodate his needs."

"Brothers for life." The Giggler, aka Bruce, releases his rope, and the net lands on the deer carcass with an audible splat. "Great mens of the forest."

"This is the downside to the formation of an alternative society," Featherhair says with what seems like real regret.

Braidbeard spits a loogie in Bruce's general direction. "In Sparta, they killed the weak," he says.

"Can you walk?" Featherhair asks, ignoring Braidbeard as he leans down to inspect my gore-smeared legs.

"This isn't my blood," I say.

Yivi takes an assertive step forward. Her knife wavers in her fist. "Who the fuck are you guys?" she asks.

"Nobody special," Featherhair says with a small smile. "Some folks call us *the White Tribe*; others prefer *Friends of Tomorrow.* Our name is less important, however, than your departure. This is a dangerous place at night, especially for outsiders. I recommend the two of you leave our forest before it gets dark."

"We're lost," I say, and Bruce giggles.

Braidbeard nods. "You sure as shit are."

"And I don't trust this Bruce guy not to follow us," I say.

"We'll handle our friend." Featherhair points off to my left. "The main road is roughly three miles that way." He turns and strides back in the direction they came, as if our interaction has come to its logical conclusion.

Bruce stares at Yivi with an almost childlike curiosity as Braidbeard begins to herd him back toward the hovels.

"What about your *dad*, babe?" Yivi asks, and I flinch. I consider lunging sideways and clamping a hand over her mouth. She is still wielding her knife, but her vibe has changed. Calm, curious, playful—a perfect reversion to her normal meddling self. "You should ask these wild-ass dudes if he lives with them," she continues.

I stare at the tip of Braidbeard's kitchen-knife spear. I shouldn't test our luck, but Yivi's right. Between the shit Mom said and everything I know about my father, it'd actually be weirder if these dudes hadn't met him.

"Wait a sec, guys," I say. "I don't mean to pry, but do either of you happen to know an old redheaded dude who talks way too much and believes white people are descended from an ancient alien race called *the Vril*?"

"We know a lot of guys like that," Braidbeard says after a brief hesitation.

"Are any of them named Henry Gunderson?" I ask.

Featherhair stops and exchanges glances with his companion. Neither seems sure what to say, and a silent debate passes between them. Patience isn't necessarily one of my virtues, but I keep my mouth shut while they figure whatever they're figuring.

"Why do you want to know?" Featherhair asks, finally.

"My mom told me my father might live out here in this forest, and I just thought—"

"It's possible," Braidbeard says, "but we can't help you."

"Alright," I say. "Cool." The more I get to know them, the more I'm beginning to think these guys are only slightly saner than Bruce, and while I'm sort of beginning to wish I could see my father again, if only to apologize, I'd rather not meet any more of his buddies.

"No, babe," Yivi says, throwing up her hands. "It's not fucking *cool*. We drove all the way here from Chicago, and we walked through this whole stupid forest, and we almost died like sixteen times, and *then* we got traumatized by this freaky naked dude, so if there's even a teeny-*tiny* chance you guys know where my friend's dad is, then the literal *least* you can do is take us to him."

"Chance or not," Braidbeard says as he shifts the rusty tip of his spear toward Yivi, "it's against our rules to let outsiders enter our sacred territory."

"Then I guess you're gonna have to make an exception," Yivi says, waving her knife to punctuate every word. She raises her feisty bleached eyebrows at me. "Am I right?"

Fucking hell, Yivi. I suppress a grin. It's hard not to admire her fearlessness, especially given her total lack of a legitimate criminal history. I wish I could send her back to Hookville on her own, but I'd worry too much. And there's no way I can survive this journey without her. "She's right," I say, after deciding there might be something more hydrating than rum in these dudes' sacred territory. "Only fools make rules, and I don't give two shits about yours."

TEN

After our final Thanksgiving, I quit speaking to my father, but he didn't quit speaking to me. The calls kept coming. The rambling texts and the unfunny memes. Jenny told me I should block his number, but I never did, and I'd be lying if I said I didn't listen to his voicemails.

He liked to call around noon on workdays, usually to warn me about impending Chinese invasions or to remind me to utilize the Law of Attraction. When COVID started shutting down cities, he begged me to stock up on food. On January 6th, he told me he was there and fighting for freedom. He joined a Texas militia, hunted sex traffickers, and patrolled the Rio Grande. He met the real man behind QAnon and claimed he wasn't impressed. I don't know if any of this shit really happened, but I followed along because, to be honest, I was lonely. And he's my father. Maybe some such men are replaceable, but mine is one of a kind. I have often hoped his ramblings might contain lessons that could help me cope with adulthood. Life hurts more than ever these days, and it's possible I'm not as smart or woke as I think I am. Despite my best efforts, I worry about fluoride in the water supply, I'm pretty sure Ted Cruz and Ron DeSantis are reptiles, I fear Sharia laws only slightly less than Christian ones, and I would love to attribute systemic global injustices to an elite group of hyperwealthy puppeteers. Some small percentage of conspiracy theories must be true, and it seems unwise to disregard every single one of them simply because the accompanying websites make a fortune selling sugar pills. The truth, I hope, is out there, and my father is one of the few people I've ever met who cares enough to search.

Unfortunately, that search is exhausting. In the end, the real reason I stopped talking to my father had more to do with time than it did with our fight. I was too busy, and his constant paranoia was making me anxious and wasting my energy. The future I imagined only seemed possible if I focused on my work. Successful people don't spend their days talking to failed old men. So, yeah, he called, and I stayed silent. Sometimes I'd hear his voice in the background while I was talking to Mom, and I'd almost ask her to hand him the phone, but I never did. And then, roughly two years ago, he stopped calling.

Without his name illuminating my phone screen, a great weight lifted from my life. I wasn't happy, but I was free to be unhappy on my own terms. Free to fear my own fears and gradually reinvent myself however I chose. In hindsight, that reinvention didn't exactly go as planned. Time has passed, but I am the same asshole who threw those punches, and this dipshit country is hurtling toward the same horrific conclusion. I thought my father had given up, but now that I know he merely relocated to the wilderness, I am beginning to regret the decision to end our relationship the same way I regret asking these dudes in robes to help me find him. I doubt this will be a happy reunion, and my optimism is flagging. We've been walking for at least an hour, and the temperature has increased to a level normally reserved for cremations.

"I think I'm dying of thirst," Yivi says.

"Not the mildest day to get lost in our woods," Featherhair replies, though he and his companion appear relatively unfazed. "But rest assured we have plenty of water where we're headed—provided you don't mind drinking straight from the Earth."

"I'd drink three gallons of hot pee right now if I could," Yivi says.

"I feel you, dude," I say. "I'd drink curdled blood from an ugly baby."

Yivi snickers, and we both break into dumb and hallucinatory laughter.

"Just think, babe," Yivi says, when she's regained herself. "If it weren't for you, I'd still be chilling in basement AC right now."

"Yeah, well . . ." I glance at the sky as another reddish bird glides through a break in the branches. "If it weren't for *you*, I'd probably be dead."

"Don't put that shit on me," Yivi says, and her eyes narrow, disappearing into grayish smudges of mascara.

"Our own pain is our own fault," Braidbeard says, marching behind us.

"Cool opinion," I mutter, and the red-winged bird swoops past us again, probably circling in case I decide to abort this mission and kill myself. Kidding aside, I lack the guts for suicide. Jenny was always the brave one, and for some reason, I don't actually want to die. I wish I did. That would be easier than wanting to live but not knowing how. Death is a great simplifier. And the idea of rotting into the dirt sounds more relaxing than getting sober. That said, I've never understood my own preoccupation with dying. I didn't know my grandparents, aunts, or uncles well enough to mourn them when they passed, and before Jenny, death was not a specter looming over my days. Maybe that's my problem. If Henry Gunderson had died when I was young the way his father did, my memories could have been more pleasant. Or maybe they're as pleasant as anyone's. Maybe the bad helps me appreciate the better. Times I felt calm knowing my father was working. Times I felt safe knowing he would kill anyone who tried to hurt us. Times I felt loved knowing my father wanted, more than anything, to share his admittedly unique perspective with me.

"He asked you a question, babe," Yivi says, bumping me with her hip.

"Who did?"

Featherhair has fallen into step alongside me. "I asked you why you're looking for your father."

"I have something important to tell him," I say.

Yivi tilts her head. "You good, babe?"

"I think your Q is making me nostalgic." I reach into my shorts and extract the remaining pills that have been rattling around in my pocket. "Want one?"

"Oh shit," Yivi says. "I meant to tell you earlier, but there's no such thing as Q."

I jiggle the tiny red pellets in my palm. "But I thought your dad was a psychiatrist."

"He is, babe—but those are just Red Hots."

"Rejoice, young travelers," Featherhair says, thrusting his hands above his head. "We have reached the edge of our sacred territory."

Bewildered, I inspect the trees, shrubs, rocks, everything, without finding any clear evidence of sacredness. "How can you tell?" I ask.

"Father Earth speaks through us," Featherhair says. "And to you, He says, *Welcome.*"

Yivi and I hobble into the bustling camp the White Tribe calls home, and the words *sacred* and *territory* continue to seem like an overpromise. Instead, words like *favela* and *shantytown* come to mind. Also: *meth lab.*

"That building over there is the Great Hall," Featherhair says, pointing with an untrimmed fingernail at a saggy white farmhouse that could use a new roof. "And that's Freedom Town," he continues, redirecting his nasty-boy fingernail toward a tumbledown barn with a giant white *W* painted on the side. Around the barn, several clusters of tents, lean-tos, teepees, and makeshift sheds form a much larger version of the migrant camps you can find under overpasses in Chicago.

"How many people live here?" Yivi asks.

"Sometimes more, sometimes less," Featherhair says. "Depending on the season."

The main encampment occupies the center of a clear-cut lot surrounded by forest. I lack the ability to estimate acreage, but the clearing is big, several football fields in diameter. Mud paths and wild grass take up most of the nonresidential space, and what look like gardens and fenced-in animal pens fill the rest. The bottom of the sun has dipped beneath the treetops, and the field is alive with shadows. White men in white robes hustle about, attending to chores: farming and building and making fires. Aside from the few instances of modern construction and a handful of brightly colored tents, even the Amish seem more contemporary than these dudes.

Yivi's eager eyes are aflame, perceiving without believing. "I have so many questions," she says.

"I'm sure you do," Featherhair says. "And I hope you understand why we can't give you details about our lifestyle."

"We're already gonna get whupped just for bringing y'all here," Braidbeard says.

"*Whupped?*" I ask.

"Y'all better have some water before we get you settled." Featherhair leads us over to an old red water pump sticking out of the ground, and Yivi drops to her knees near the spout.

"Pump for me, babe?"

"Are you guys sure this shit is safe to drink?" I ask, grabbing the handle and working my tired arms until brackish water shoots directly into Yivi's eyes. She sputters, eventually locating the stream with her mouth.

"Safer than the toxic sludge in your world," Braidbeard says.

"My bad for asking," I say as Yivi and I switch places. I drink deeply from the pump. Room temp and metallic, but better than expected. When I'm finished, my shirt is soaked and my stomach is sloshing, but I feel a tad less hungover, and for the first time in weeks, I'm kind of hungry.

Featherhair claps his hands together. "Has Father Earth's glorious lifeblood renewed your strength?"

"If I die today, it won't be of dehydration," I say, shifting my attention back to the compound. Some of the men have noticed our presence. They're gawking, and not necessarily in a friendly way.

"Let's get a move on." Braidbeard lifts me off my knees and shoves me back toward the footpath. "We've gotta put y'all somewhere safe while we powwow the Chief."

We march through the campground on a collision course with Freedom Town, and most of the men stop what they're doing and stare. They look famished. Hungrier than me. We're a long way from Waffle House, and I certainly wouldn't eat anything grown or raised by these dudes. Yellowing leaves hang limply from cornstalks, a small herd of malnourished cows wanders around a corral on the verge of collapse, and several chickens make noises that don't sound happy or healthy. We're approaching a small, brownish stream that runs along the perimeter of Freedom Town, and I am starting to regret drinking from whatever well feeds that water pump.

"Hurry now," Braidbeard says as we hustle past a totem pole depicting the crudely carved faces of several unattractive white men. "We're almost there."

"This is as fast as I can walk," Yivi says.

I lift my knees to keep pace. "We're basically jogging."

Aside from the totem pole, I spy countless more instances of these men's delusions and derangements. Nazi flags hang from clotheslines, and a wooden sign proclaims THIS IS THE DAY OF THE ROPE. Suddenly I am extremely worried for Yivi's safety. And mine. I doubt the sentiment around here is pro-queer. That said, the total lack of women gives me pause. My father has never exuded anything resembling gay energy, and it's unlikely that he would go full *Beginners* if given the chance, but that man is brimming with surprises. The alt-right's obsession with genitals is probably the queerest thing on the internet, and while I'm not an expert, I'm pretty sure incels take what they can get.

As if on cue, a heavyset 4chan-forum of a man wielding a garden hoe steps in front of us on the path, blocking our way. His mole-like eyes flick between Yivi and me, as if he can't decide whether we're real. "What gives, Bob?" the heavyset man asks, apparently addressing Featherhair.

"Visitors for the chief," Braidbeard says, continuing down the path.

Featherhair-Bob stops to speak with the heavyset man, and I hear him use the words *special circumstances.*

"I'm starting to worry we might not be extremely welcome here," I say.

"Far as I'm concerned, you aren't," Braidbeard says.

"Are you guys really gonna get in trouble?" Yivi asks, and Braidbeard ignores her.

We speedwalk in silence past a tent with a DON'T TREAD ON ME banner safety pinned to its side before coming to a halt outside a dome-like hut.

"What's this thing?" Yivi asks, inspecting the curved doorway of the hut, which is much better constructed than the dilapidated hovels where Bruce was hanging out. Clearly the handiwork of a much more experienced craftsman.

"Wigwam," Braidbeard says, ushering us inside.

"We're all supposed to live in houses like these," Featherhair-Bob says as he catches up with us. "But we're still learning how to build them."

"This Indian shit ain't easy," Braidbeard says, disappearing into the interior darkness and bumping around until artificial light fills the wigwam.

I stand in awe as my eyes adjust. Everywhere, hand-painted writing covers the curved walls. Strange white letters. I read the familiar phrases.

WAKE UP NOW

FEAR NO EVIL

FOOLS MAKE RULES

TRUST NO ONE

WARRIORS NOT WORRIERS
THE PAST IS A LIE
MAY THE BLESSINGS BE

Yivi shuffles closer to the wall with her head cranked upward. "Who wrote all this stuff?"

"My father did," I say as Braidbeard hands me the Coleman lantern he's using to illuminate the space. "This must be my father's house."

Featherhair-Bob and Braidbeard leave us to wait in the wigwam. A pair of upturned plastic buckets form makeshift chairs near a small wooden table, and Yivi and I decide to rest our legs. We sit, catching our breath and reading the walls. I lack the desire to explain any of this, and Yivi can tell.

Aside from my father's scribbled rantings, the wigwam contains a few more semi-pathetic signs of life. A pile of coarse blankets lies against one wall, a series of clay pots lines the shelves of a handmade bookcase, and a workbench near the door is covered with some of my father's old hand tools. More tools hang from the wall above the workbench, and even in the low light, I can see letters on the handles.

HG.

HG.

HG.

My father's initials—and my own. When I was a kid, he liked to insist that all his tools were as much mine as his. He hadn't wanted me to become a carpenter, but he wanted to make sure I could take care of myself. Another project he may or may not have failed to complete.

"I wonder where your dad is?" Yivi says when she has clearly gotten bored of my performative tranquility.

"I bet he'll be along shortly."

"Are you nervous?"

"Maybe," I say, before deciding she deserves more than my moody reticence. "Are you?"

"Why would *I* be nervous?"

"Because these white supremacists might eat us."

Yivi snorts, apparently under the impression that I was making a joke. "I don't think they're gonna *eat* us, babe. It's more likely they'll chain us to a wall and use us as sex slaves."

"You don't find that nerve-racking?"

"Your dad won't let that happen."

"Good point," I say, though I wish I had her confidence. "Can I ask you something?"

"Of course."

"Do you see now why I stopped talking to my father?"

Yivi taps a finger against her lips. "I only know what you've told me. And you haven't told me a whole lot. But this house is pretty wild. And he sounds . . . interesting."

"Interesting?"

"Passionate."

"That's one way to put it."

"If you want the truth, I kinda imagine him like you."

"He's nothing like me."

"Is he intense and funny and thoughtful and smart and crazy and infuriating?"

"He's some of those things more than others."

Yivi flashes her chipmunk grin. "Does he make you love him as much as you hate him?"

"Yivi."

"Not saying, just saying."

"I don't appreciate the implication."

"Why not?"

"Because I don't live in a freaky commune, and I'm not completely fucking insane."

"Nobody said you were insane. And it's not weird to have stuff in common with your parents. It might be the shittiest thing about being alive, but me and my dad are kinda similar sometimes—and I left home just like my mom did."

"That doesn't mean you're the same."

"But I'd be lying if I told you I wasn't my parents' kid, and I know you hate liars."

"I certainly do."

"Then maybe stop lying to *yourself*, babe."

I stand and stretch before limping across the wigwam. I reach the workbench and heft one of my father's hammers—a Craftsman framer with a silver head and a rubberized red grip. This one has the *HG* written on the claw. I swing it around, testing the weight. It's a much better weapon than a baseball bat. I've always wondered why construction needs to be so violent. Destroying old things to make new ones. My father and his tools. I guess he still brings them everywhere. Prepper impulses. He packed far too much gear for our road trip out west, but it proved useful when we had to repair Mom's Odyssey at 4:00 A.M. on our way back from Idaho.

I don't love to dwell on this because, like so many other things, it feels like my fault, but we got into a pretty serious accident driving home that night. I was anxious to get back to Chicago, worried Clinton was cheating, and I pushed my father to leave in the evening rather than wait until dawn. We'd spent the last week and a half hopping between cheap motels, and we hadn't slept much or well. I drove us south through Boise, and my father took over in Wyoming. I don't remember falling asleep against my door, but I remember waking up.

Holden, my father said, and something hit me hard across the chest. I opened my eyes. A moose stood in the center of the road. My father was bracing me with his arm. He should've kept both hands on the wheel. The creature was massive, tall enough to stare down at me through the windshield. Awash in our headlights, the antlers shone like weapons from another world. I remember believing I was about to die, and I also remember a frantic desire to live. My father swerved into the other lane, and we hit the moose with the rear passenger-side door. It nearly totaled the Odyssey. When we finally stopped spinning and the minivan found its way into a roadside gulch, my father's arm was still pressed against my chest.

"You sure you're up to this, babe?" Yivi asks.

I swing the Craftsman hammer at her question. A rusty DeWalt hacksaw dangles from a hook at eye level. I grab it with my free hand and dual wield the tools. "I see, said the blind carpenter," I say.

Yivi frowns, clearly alarmed. "Are you having a stroke?"

"It's my father's favorite joke."

"What is?"

"*I see*, said the blind carpenter, as he picked up his hammer and *saw*."

She doesn't seem impressed. "I get it," she says.

"It's not super funny."

"How can the carpenter see if he's blind?"

"Blue-collar magic." I return the tools to their hooks and walk the perimeter of the wigwam, running my fingers along the well-thatched walls. When I was very young, I used to get a strange pleasure whenever my father would slice a long piece of plywood on his table saw and I'd trace the fresh-cut edge with my fingertips, sniffing the pine and relishing the smoothness. My main responsibility was pushing sawdust into piles with the shop broom my father had stolen from a jobsite. He would whistle while we worked, and I enjoyed his off-tune songs. They seemed to come from far away or long ago. I can't remember the last time I heard anyone whistling. I also can't remember the last time I listened.

"Why'd you run away from home, Yivi?" I ask, returning to the bucket stool next to hers.

"Cuz I needed to."

"That's the *only* reason?"

"I dunno, babe." Yivi makes a face I can't quite parse. "Why'd you quit your job, leave your boyfriend, and take a completely nonsensical vow of honesty?"

"Because I needed to."

Yivi smiles. "Period." She studies my broken face for a stretch. "I needed to get away from my dad," she says finally. "So I decided to look for my mom."

"In Chicago?"

"Obviously not." She glances away as embarrassment stains her cheeks. "I basically only got off there because I freaked out on the Amtrak."

"Did somebody try to fuck with you?"

She scrapes a line into the dirt floor with the toe of her boot. "I just didn't know how or where to start looking. My dad took away my phone before I left, and I was basically broke. I stole his credit card, but I was afraid to buy anything cuz I figured he'd track me down. I was eventually forced to book that Airbnb, and I guess that's how the cowboy detective lady found me. I was pretty sure that'd happen, but I didn't wanna give up. I had this idea that I was gonna completely reinvent myself and live outside of society. As if I could escape it, you know? Like, sometimes I get this feeling that I don't have a real future. College and all that. It's pretty bleak if you're paying attention. There aren't gonna be jobs, and the world is boiling, and college means debt, and AI is coming, blah, blah, blah. You shouldn't get married. You shouldn't have kids. The economy is gonna collapse, Trump's gonna find a way to be president forever, and the Supreme Court is basically perma-fucked. It's scary, babe, but nobody ever wants to talk about how scary it is. Most of my bitch-ass classmates are just fucking around on TikTok, you know?"

"It *is* scary, Yivi."

"I hate it." She draws a V in the dirt with her boot, turning her original line into a Y. "And thanks for calling me Yivi."

"What else would I call you?"

"My real name."

"You'll always be Yivi to me." I wrap my arm around her shoulders. She leans against me, and I hold her for a while. I'm worried she might cry. Instead, she starts playing with her cat-head necklace. She holds it out and flips it over.

"Look at this dummy shit," she says, showing me the back of the cat. Next to the tail, there's a teeny row of all-caps black letters. A single word.

"YIVI," I say, making a tremendous effort not to laugh. "Is that the *brand*?"

"This is the first thing I ever stole."

"Your maiden voyage to the land of Kleptomania."

Yivi tucks the necklace into the collar of my father's Panama Jack shirt. "It's silly, but I've always thought it'd be a cool name."

"It *is* a cool name." I squeeze her shoulder. Then something catches my ear. "Do you hear that?"

"Hear what?"

"That music." From a long way off comes a high-pitched whistling. Pleasantly out of tune. I release Yivi's shoulder and turn to face the wigwam door.

"I think so," she says.

What feels like a full minute passes, and the song grows louder. I stand and dust the day off my clothes.

"You think that's him?" Yivi asks as several sets of footsteps join the whistling.

"Might be."

"Are you ready for this?" she asks, but before I can answer, Featherhair-Bob steps through the doorway.

"Sorry we kept you waiting," he says, turning aside so another man can enter the wigwam. "The chief was taking a nap."

"Holden goddamn Gunderson!" says a short man with a hangdog face and thin gray hair. "What the heck are you doing all the way out here?"

"Is this your dad?" Yivi asks as the short man limps toward us.

"Definitely not," I say. "This must be the chief."

"You're both wrong," the short man says, smiling with yellow teeth. "And truth be told, I'm disappointed you don't remember me."

"Have we met?" I ask.

The short man gives Featherhair-Bob a sheepish smile. "Guess it's been longer than I thought." The hem of his white robe drags on the ground as he hobbles closer and extends his hand. I reach for it, realizing as our palms slap that he's missing a thumb.

"Holy shit," I say, recognizing the dark nub of knuckle. "Chuck!"

"Now he sees me," Chuck Steinbacher says, wrapping me in an awkward hug. "I knew this kid when he was barely half a sprout." He holds me longer than I would prefer before stepping back to appraise my sorry condition. "What the butt-ugly *hell* happened to your face?" he asks, his Chicago accent clattering around the wigwam like Al Capone's tommy gun.

"I thought you were dead," I say.

"Nope, nope—not dead." Chuck's eyes twinkle the way they used to whenever he was pouring me a drink. "Though I did spread that news around for a while so I could stop paying taxes."

"My parents said it was liver failure, I think."

"Would've made sense, back then, but not these days. I'm sober seven years, and there's not much temptation in the camp. That's one of the reasons I originally came out here. Seems so long ago, I almost forget I used to live like that."

I nod because I can't think of anything to say. It's an odd thing, seeing a ghost, but I shouldn't be surprised. When it comes to my father, the mysteries are endless. "Where is he?" I ask, when I realize I don't actually care how or why Chuck ended up here.

"Your dad?" Chuck bobs his head from side to side. "Well, kid, I'm sorry I've gotta be the one to tell you, but your old man is no longer with us."

"What?" I ask. "Since when?"

"A week ago. Maybe two?" Chuck's droopy face droops even lower. "I swear, kid. You just missed him."

"You mean he *left*?"

"He died, Holden," Chuck says. "He's gone."

The wigwam does a barrel roll, and Yivi grabs my arm. I can tell Chuck isn't joking, but some part of me hopes this might be a prank. Featherhair-Bob lurks near the doorway, staring at the floor. Suddenly, I am furious.

"WHY THE FUCK DID YOU BRING ME ALL THE WAY OUT HERE IF YOU KNEW HE WAS *DEAD*?!" I ask. "WHY THE FUCK DIDN'T YOU TELL ME?!"

"When I saw the state of your face and your clothes, I figured you'd come a long, hard way to see him." Featherhair-Bob clasps his hands, continuing to hang his head. "And I wanted to give you the chance to say goodbye."

"I'm sorry you had to find out like this, Holden."

"Their name's not Holden anymore, Mr. Chuck," Yivi says. "And you're gonna have to excuse them for yelling. They're having a pretty shitty couple of weeks."

"Are you his girlfriend?" Chuck asks with far too much cordiality for my taste. "I didn't catch your name."

"I'm . . ." She hesitates. "I'm Yivi."

"Nice to meet you, Yivi." Chuck shakes her hand, and I'd like to punch him.

I draw a few shallow breaths, attempting to regain my composure. "Did one of these assholes kill him, Chuck?"

"No, kid. His heart just quit out in the field one day. It was all over pretty quick."

"I'm so fucking sorry, babe," Yivi whispers, and I glance at the ceiling. Directly above me, nestled into the curved peak of the wigwam, I find the words MAKE SURE YOU DIE SCREAMING, and I come excruciatingly close to laughing.

"Was there a funeral?" I ask.

"He was recycled," Featherhair-Bob says, as if this is a

perfectly reasonable alternative. "But you can still say goodbye to his bones."

"Is that supposed to be funny?" I ask.

"Would you like to see them?" Chuck asks, using his sole thumb to point backward over his shoulder.

"We'd love to see them," Yivi says, tugging me by the hand until I follow.

"Sure, Chuck," I say, completely defeated. "Take me to the bones."

Time flies, I guess. Night fell without my noticing, and a nearly full moon haunts the sky from behind a curtain of clouds, lending an unsettling bluish hue to the mismatched tents and their ghostly residents. Everywhere, campfires flicker. Men laugh and shout. The musty smell of overcooked meat drifts on the breeze.

We follow Chuck through the camp. He lights our way with my father's Coleman lantern. Yivi wraps her arm around my waist. She pulls me close. I appreciate her concern, but my father made his choices. We both did.

"He's right up here," Chuck says, his white robe billowing as the wind gusts and the temperature drops to a more tolerable degree. We pass a cluster of gaunt men weaving turkey feathers into their hair while they debate intelligent design, and their conversation falls to whispers.

"Hey, Chuck," I say after a long period of silence. "Would you mind explaining what's going on in this place? Like, what's the appeal?"

For several paces, Chuck meditates on my question. I hope my asking didn't offend him. Yivi and I will need his help getting out of this forest, and I'm not about to trust anyone else here.

"I don't want to speak for everyone," Chuck says, leading us across a rustic wooden bridge. "And I certainly don't want to speak for Hank, but I think it's about feeling less alone. All these boys felt pretty lost before they got here. I know I did. Your dad was the one who told me about this place, but I joined up first. I couldn't handle that shithole liars' world anymore. And I was dying. The drinking was one thing, but I also couldn't make a living. I couldn't compete with all those fucking illegals, and a couple quacks told me I needed back surgery if I wanted to keep working. One young Muslim asshole said there was a 50-percent chance they'd need to fuse my spine together, and then what the fuck? My insurance wouldn't even cover a *quarter* of the procedure. If I didn't want the surgery, the only solution anyone could give me was take these pills and OD my way into permanent retirement. That's a common story around here. Some of these guys were homeless before they joined us, and some were just running from the Feds or that goddamn COVID nonsense, but now they're safe. They've got warm food and a whole brotherhood looking after them. My back's stopped hurting most of the time, and I like living off the land the way real men are supposed to. It feels good."

"Do you think my father was happy here?" I ask as we approach a wooden fence forming an animal pen around a newly constructed shed.

"Happy as a pig in shit." Chuck stops to hang the Coleman lantern from a hook. "It's nice to be around these guys who believe what we believe, you know?" Chuck turns to appraise me, and he must notice something pitiful spoiling my face. "But don't get me wrong," Chuck continues, "your dad missed his family. He mentioned you and your brother all the time—bragging you up like big shots doing big things. Some folks got pretty sick of hearing it, but you know how he was. You couldn't shut that man's mouth if you tried."

"That's the truth," I say.

Chuck chuckles, shaking his head. "Hank was Hank." He steps up to the fence, and a squeaky chorus rises to greet him. A large brown pig shoves its snout through the slats, and a noisy litter of piglets swarms the bigger pig's legs. It's all very adorable—until I notice the grayish bones of a human skeleton half-buried in the mud.

"Whoa, babe," Yivi says, leaning forward over the fence. "Is that your *dad*?"

Chuck unhooks a gate. "And the wheel turns." He steps gingerly across the pen, lifting the hem of his robe to save it from the sludge. The stench is wild, but nothing compares to the visual: an old carpenter pretending to be a Native American as he pulls my dead father's skull from the pig-shitty muck. "Hope you're peaceful, old buddy," he says.

I grab my dad's damp cranium between my fingertips, avoiding the spots where poop clings to the cheekbones. It's just half a skull, really. The pigs were thorough with their dismemberment, and the jawbone must be somewhere in the mud. I stare into the place where his nose should be, a dark and empty hole, and suddenly, the sky above us explodes.

"What the fuck is that?" I ask, following the light as the pigs start to scream.

"Fireworks," Yivi says as a pair of red and furious spiderwebs dance across the sky, shimmering high above the silent trees. The sparks fall and dim, but moments later, the red is joined by blue, then white.

"There's a big sporting lake over that way," Chuck says. "And I guess it's the Fourth."

"I didn't even realize it was July," I say.

"Wow." Yivi laughs. "Me neither."

"Guess we're closer to the real world than I thought," I say, but Chuck only shrugs.

"America's everywhere, kids," he says. "The best we can do is ignore it."

Yivi rests her head on my shoulder. "You can run but you can't hide," she says.

"So it goes." Chuck watches the sky. "By the way, what are you calling yourself these days besides *Holden*?" he asks.

"HG," I say without hesitation. "I shortened it to the initials."

"I dig it." Chuck stomps mud off his moccasins as he exits the pigpen. "Let me know when you're finished saying goodbye." He places his palms together as he bends at the waist, dipping into a culturally confusing bow. "Take your time," he says before slouching off toward Freedom Town.

"You okay, babe?" Yivi whispers, after a moment.

"Not really."

"Do you want some time alone with the skull?"

I break into a grin that stings my swollen nose. "That's literally the craziest question anyone's ever asked me."

"I felt pretty silly just saying it."

I shove my father's filthy remains near Yivi's face. "Say hello to Henry Gunderson."

"*Stop!*" She recoils, covering her mouth to stifle her cackling. "You're deranged."

"Maybe I am." I flick a maggot nibbling one of my father's earholes. "But you've gotta give me the benefit of the doubt because this isn't exactly how I'd imagined my family reunion."

"How'd you imagine it?"

"A lot more shouting."

Another firework sparkles in Yivi's dark eyes. "Are you still angry?"

"Who knows," I say. The anger is there, but I can't feel the heat. In truth, I can't feel much. Essential things like what I believe and what I am and what I'll do next seem oddly far away, and I'm not even drunk. A small miracle.

Yivi fidgets with her cat-head necklace. "It's okay if you are."

"What's funny is I'm trying to remember the last time he and I spoke," I say. "But I keep remembering it wrong."

"How do you remember it now?"

"We had a fight, but it wasn't really over politics." I rotate the skull, inspecting the jagged ridges and porcine bite marks by the light of the bombs bursting in air. "He said he was worried I'd forgotten who I was, and I got pissed because I hadn't forgotten. I just couldn't figure out how to do it. And I think that shit was his fault. Or at least the fault of guys like him."

"I get that," Yivi says.

I raise the skull and position it next to my cheek, stretching my eyelids wide to match the empty sockets. "Can you see the family resemblance?"

"It's uncanny."

"To cry or not to cry," I say, turning my father's head so I'm meeting his dead-guy gaze. "That's the *real* question."

"There's something so severely wrong with you."

"Duh." I dab the corner of my eye with my wrist. "Let's go and bury my dad."

We wade out into a low field of flowering green vines. Tomatoes maybe. The fireworks continue overhead, an ostentatious showing for such a remote corner of flyover country, but I'm no longer interested in America's birthday bombs aside from their utility as a light source.

"Are you really gonna start going by HG?" Yivi asks as I fumble around in the dark.

"Of course not," I say. "It sounds terrible."

"You said it, not me."

"The initials are just a placeholder until I figure out another name that starts with *H*." I stop and drop to my knees in a patch of soil where the flowering plants aren't growing. "Here looks good," I say.

"I agree, HG." Yivi patronizes my back with a comforting palm. "Here seems great."

I plunge my fingernails into the earth. I dig for a few minutes in silence, and it isn't easy. My whole body is overcome with exhaustion. I need to start exercising, eating right, living for more than the next whatever. And maybe I will. Maybe I'll stay at Mom's place for a while. She seems willing to change, and we could both use the company. I'll call my brother and get his ass over here from England. Meet some of his kids. Rebuild our strange, broken family.

I toss one last handful of dirt off to the side. My dad's skull looks tiny when I place it into the hole. Ashes to ashes, dirt to dirt, him to me. Maybe. Without the jawbone, it's hard to picture his massive mouth, but I can still hear his voice in my head. "Stay screaming, Dad."

"Here. Wait." Yivi squats and unzips her fannypack. "Don't laugh," she says, laying her mom's postcard next to the skull.

I study the wrinkled paper. The gleaming arch. WESTWARD HO! "You sure about this, Yiv?"

"Yeah, babe. It's time."

"You're right," I say, fighting like hell to hold my shit together.

With shaky fingers, I remove my wallet from my pocket. It takes a sec to wriggle my Chili's gift card free from its leather slot. When I do, I drop it between my dad's skull and Yivi's postcard. This might be the dumbest thing I've ever done, but it feels right, and Yivi doesn't ask. I appreciate that.

"Goodbye," Yivi says, and I say it too. Goodbye and goodbye. Tears crawl my cheeks as I refill the hole. I straighten and stomp it flat. Yivi helps. Then she hugs me. Hard. I hold her while she cries, and my thoughts drift back to the future. It's true that this country is fucked, but I refuse to let it fuck me gently. I'm no hero, I'll never be a winner, and I barely have a name, but with Yivi by my side, I feel like somebody, and somebody needs to do something about all this terrible everything.

"Hey, Yivi," I say, when her sobs cease and her breathing slows. "Whatever happens next, I just want to say I'm glad I met you. I know you're basically a kid, and I know you probably need to go home and deal with your shitty dad, but I love you like a sister. You might not realize this, but you single-handedly got me through the worst few weeks of my life. If you ever need anything, I don't care what it is, I'm here. I've got your back. And if I never hear from you again after tomorrow, that's okay. I'll still be happy knowing that somewhere out there I have a psychic, communist, knife-wielding, drug-dealing, and huge-hearted garbage-goth friend named Yivi."

A big blue firework pops overhead, giving Yivi's hair a haunting sheen. Her eyes dart around before locating mine. We stare, and she smirks. "But that's only like half-true," she says.

"I know," I say as the last firework dies, and we both disappear into the darkness. "But it's the half I choose to believe in."